AN UNEXPECTED
BREW

To An
Awesome library :)

J.E.Mueller

Published 2018 by J.E.Mueller
Cover by Ravenborn
Book formatting by Lia at Free Your Words

ISBN: 978-1721808304

This novel is dedicated to:
TWC Discord

Usually a chat group is more distracting than not,
But you've all been a blessing on this silly project.

Extra shout-out to:

@Steph @Jasper @Nichole @NolaSong
@AudasaurusRex

CHAPTER 1

Before the sun could fully rise, I was up. Yawning as I turned on this light and that machine, I began the morning prep for my family's coffee shop. It was a routine I could easily do in my zombie-like state – a routine I had followed for far too many years.

I had loved when Father bought this shop. It was a new beginning for us after Mother passed away. Something exciting and fun – a new adventure for our smaller family, even if at the time I was too young to use all the machines.

Then *she* came in.

I wouldn't say Henrietta was a cruel woman. I wouldn't say that she was lovely either. In fact, the only thing I could say with certainty was that she loved her daughters and money – and not in that order.

At first, I refused to call her Mother. Then I saw how much it irked her to call her such and did so with glee. Mother Dearest couldn't say a word against it since it made my father so happy.

Then he got sick, too.

It was a hard couple of months once father became ill, and we thought he would have this cancer beat. It wasn't meant to be.

That winter, almost spring, we laid him to rest. Henrietta assumed full control of the shop, and I assumed full responsibility for the morning shift, the ordering, the stock, and everything but the book-keeping and hiring. Henrietta knew numbers and how to strike fear into the rest of the staff, save her daughters. They were pretty and giggly, but neither could figure out how to steam milk, let alone brew a simple cup of coffee.

Diamond, the eldest of the two, knew all about shoes and the latest fashions. Which was great, except she spent more time fixing her makeup and modeling for the customers than learning how to do her job. Rose had the singing voice of an angel, which could make the job fun if she wasn't usually creating a bigger mess for us. Thankfully, Rose had few shifts since she was still in high school. The rest of the work crew learned quickly to ignore them if they wanted to keep their job. The regulars also either ignored them or came just to see them.

This wasn't some ugly step-sister story. Both of them could have had modeling careers if they wanted. They had pretty hair, currently dyed in the latest rose-gold trend, and darling amber eyes that seemed to sparkle just right whenever a cute guy entered. Diamond even had the height thing going for her, though Rose had more of the delicate and soft ballerina look working for her.

Rose said I could be fashionable too if I changed my hair. Diamond just laughed and said it would take too much work to make me pretty. I ignored both of them. I liked my black curls. They were cute, springy, and usually a lot of fun. Sure, looks mattered a bit to me, but what really mattered was that I had nearly saved up enough to go away to university. The local college was fine and all, but I knew the only way I'd succeed would be to leave home.

There was no way Henrietta would help with that.

She needed me here. No one else knew how to work things as well as I did. Not to mention it would take several people to cover my duties if I left. It was about time they learned how to really run this place.

So, silently I suffered on. Soon, I promised myself as I made myself a cup of coffee. Soon, I promised myself as I set up the pastry display.

Then it was time to open.

It was after ten, the morning rush nothing more than a memory now, when my step-sister, Diamond, shuffled in with a yawn. Rolling my eyes, I made her a drink while she sluggishly put her coat up and tied on her apron.

Diamond reached the front counter after a few minutes and slowly sipped her drink as I restocked the bar. "Did you make sure there's charm in this, Arnessa?" She eyed me tiredly.

"Duh," I replied flatly. "Do I look like a level one mage?"

The biggest reason our coffee shop was so successful was because of the magic we brewed into it. While neither of my sisters could make a particularly delicious drink, they were fairly well gifted in magic. Adding extra effects to drinks wasn't overly difficult. Some added charisma? Got it. Need to be extra alluring? No prob! Love spell? Well, my stepsisters swore they could, but that was beyond their skills. Truthfully, it was beyond mine as well. But who was I to say it didn't work? Sometimes that extra confidence was all you needed for your crush to notice you.

Diamond just grumbled at me and set her drink aside as a rather handsome guy walked in. Instantly, I saw her perk up. It had been three days since she had dumped her last boyfriend and she was ready for something new.

This one was exactly her type. He had great dark hair, almost a caramel brown. It was slightly long and messy, but not in a bad way. Sure, sure, he had dazzling blue eyes. I wasn't impressed. Who knew if he had magic and was just using a glamor spell? Simple glamor spells any mage could do.

"Hiya! Welcome to Magic Beans!" she greeted with a little too much enthusiasm.

The guy offered a soft smile as he reached the counter. "Morning."

"So handsome, what are we thinking to start the day with? It doesn't look like you'll need any extra boosts." She flirted unabashedly.

He chuckled but his eyes didn't leave the menu board. "What drink do you recommend? I don't want anything too bitter."

"Oh, you'd love the vanilla caramel swirl," she said with a sweet little bat of her eyelashes.

The guy didn't seem to notice. "Sure. I'll give that a shot. Maybe with a luck boost? What sort of flavor does that add?"

Diamond faltered for a moment. "Uhhh…"

"It takes the sweetness down a notch but has no noticeable flavor enhancements," I replied as I started to wipe down the back counter.

"Yep, it's just a bonus effect!" She beamed.

Handsome mystery man met her eyes. "Perfect. Can I get a medium, then?"

As she rang him up I started on his drink. While the guy walked over to the pickup counter I could hear Diamond giggle. With a glance in her direction, I saw that she was already on her phone, texting away. Likely about the gorgeous guy that was in the cafe.

Instead of paying Diamond or her newest crush any mind I went on with my task.

"Is she always like that?" I heard him say just loud enough for me to hear.

I glanced over and watched him type away on his phone. "Pretty much." I continued concentrating on the drink.

He smirked. "Well, this place still comes highly recommended. Guess it's worth a shot."

"Worth a shot?" I gave a small laugh. "Oh, you'll be back for the drinks if the girls don't scare you off."

"So certain, huh?" He had no trouble looking me in the eyes.

I handed him his drink. "Of course. I make the best drinks in town." I laughed. "Have a good one." I turned to continue cleaning, ending the conversation.

"Did you stock the condiment bar?" Diamond asked me, still giggly.

"Nope," I said looking at her. "It was fine a half hour ago. Is something wrong?" I asked surprised.

"Not at all." She smirked. I followed her gaze to the handsome guy now sitting in the cafe area.

Sighing, I went in back to start on the dishes with Steph. This was not something I wanted to deal with.

"What's up?" Steph shoved her bangs out of her eyes as I joined her.

I took note that her neatly tied back hair had somehow managed to get soap suds in it but didn't mention it. "Same old. Cute guy, overly flirty sister." I rolled my eyes.

"Does he stand a chance?" Steph sighed as she shook the remaining soap off her hands.

"He does not seem interested in Diamond, so we'll see. He might survive this visit." I noticed there wasn't enough for me to help with. Only a few dirty pitchers and a spoon remained from the previous intimidating pile.

Steph just shook her head. "This visit. Diamond can be persistent."

"Can be?" I laughed, moving to check the inventory. I'd have to make an order tomorrow.

"Fine, fine. Is stupidly persistent," Steph corrected herself as she finished the last of the dishes.

"There ya go." I winked.

"Don't you have class soon?" Steph shoved the dishes into the sanitizer and turned it on.

"Yeah, didn't realize the time. Guess that leaves you to bar. Please try not to let Di make any more drinks? Poor Kimmy and Trent got sick last week because of them," I begged as I washed my hands.

"I'll try. You know her." Steph assured me.

Nodding, I tossed my apron into the dirty bin and grabbed my stuff.

I waved to my sister as I headed out. Diamond was sulking at the register, the cute guy nowhere to be seen.

"Hey, you're going out right?" Diamond's face suddenly lit up with excitement.

"Yeah? Class as usual. Be back in about two hours." I waved again, not stopping.

"Can you find out his name?" Diamond begged.

"If I see him!" I called back, not intending to try.

To my surprise, his car was parked right next to mine and he was standing next to it while talking on his phone. I gave a wave as I opened my car door.

"Hang on, hang on…" He stated into the phone. "Barista lady! Sorry, I don't know your name."

I laughed. "It's cool. What's up?"

He seemed relieved. "I have a meeting at Cobblestone Community College, but my GPS isn't working. Can you direct me there? Or at least to a GPS friendly area?"

I had to laugh again. "That's where I'm heading. I've got class. You can follow me."

"Fantastic. You're a lifesaver." His face lit up.

"Nah, just a bit of luck. You'd have figured it out. There're signs just about everywhere. It's all this town has." I shrugged. "But, my step-sister was begging to find out your name."

"That's your sister?" He seemed surprised.

"Step-sister, and yes. The grim truth that plagues us all." I shrugged. "Anywho, just follow me."

"It's Vincent." He chuckled at my commentary.

"Awesome. Nice to meet you, Vincent." I got into my car and waited for him to get ready to follow.

Getting to the school was easy. There were only a few turns. I parked, leaving Vincent to figure out the rest of his gig as I took off for class.

I only had a few minutes to spare when I finally took my seat. My normal seat was in the middle of the stuffy room. For whatever reason, everyone always seemed to avoid the first row, and since there were only ten students in this class and about fifteen chairs that was easy to do. The whiteboard had a random drawing on it and no class notes yet so I went about getting myself ready.

My school buddy and bestie, Callie, was deep in an excited conversation with the person in front of her. As I pulled out my notebook, she looked at me.

She tossed her long silky dark hair behind her shoulder, the bangles on her arm giving a slight jingle. "Arnessa have you heard?" She excitedly giggled at me.

"Apparently not. What's up?"

Leah, the bubbly girl that was chatting with Callie, shook her head at me. "Oh come on, I know you don't care about this town but how have you not heard?"

"I live in a magical bubble called too much work," I stated flatly.

Callie shook her head as she flailed her hands in front of me so quickly I couldn't see the henna design she had recently put on them. "So, the Queen's son, you know the freaking *prince*, is in town! Apparently, he's doing several guest speakings for various classes this week and a public speaking!"

"Oh, that is actually kind of cool." I even had to wonder how I hadn't heard that one.

"You have to come to the speaking!" Callie demanded, just about ready to fall out of her chair with excitement.

"I probably have work. Let me know how it goes, though." I opened my notebook to a free page. While it would be cool to see him, it was super unlikely we'd get to actually be close to him.

"You're killing me." Callie flopped her arms down on the desk. "Oh, I heard he's speaking in a lot of the illusion classes! Maybe one of yours?"

I shrugged. "I haven't seen any announcements about guest speakers so unlikely. Unless it wasn't announced since its the prince and they wanted it to be a secret? We do get guest speakers fairly often so it's possible. They're usually more local and less celebrity status."

Callie just about shrieked with delight. "You have to tell me if you meet him!"

"I have that class tomorrow, so I'll let you know." Now that would be cool. I bet not many could say their prince helped out with a class they were in. That was a fun idea.

"Oh em gee that remin–"

The teacher walked in, cutting off Callie's next comment.

CHAPTER 2

After class Callie was all about talking again. "I wonder if he's as cute as his pictures." She gushed as I lead the way to the cafeteria.

"He specializes in illusion magic, he can be however he wants." I rolled my eyes.

"Come on, not everyone uses glamor spells," Callie pointed out. "You hardly ever use them."

"True, but if you had to keep up a wonderful public appearance, wouldn't you?" I asked simply. "It would make the most sense to use magic to your advantage when you know you have to look your best."

"I guess you have a point." Callie gave a defeated sigh.

"Nothing wrong with it, gotta do what ya gotta do to stay on your A game right?" I nudged her.

"Yeah, for real. I bet it's tough to always be camera ready," Callie shuffled along behind me. "It'll still be fun to see the speaking event. I should look up what it's about."

"If you can record it that'd be awesome," I gave her a pleading look. "I bet it'll be fun to hear."

"Sure thing." Callie followed me through the lunch line. "Healthy food or fries and pizza?"

"I'm pretty sure you've done three healthy days. Bring on the pizza," I grabbed the biggest slice available.

"And you're still doing whatever you feel like." She snickered.

"I burn too many calories working." I shrugged and took a bite before adding it to my tray.

"True..." Callie grabbed one for herself.

We were still sitting the cafeteria when Vincent came over to our table.

"It's the barista girl again." He smiled.

"Sup?" I said, reluctant to look up from my notebook. After eating I had started on my classwork.

"Just surprised to see a familiar face, though I still haven't caught your name," Vincent replied simply.

"Barista girl works." I laughed before looking back down at my notebook.

"Arnessa, you're the worst." Callie shook her head at me. "Sorry, she's actually really nice sometimes."

"Sometimes? I must be having more off days then I realize." I snickered as I jotted down some notes for the paper I would need to type up later.

"Ignore her, what was your name?" Callie asked since I hadn't bothered to introduce him.

"You can call me Vincent." He offered her a hand and she shook it, blushing fiercely.

"You can join us if you'd like. I do have class soon though, and then you'll be stuck with crabby pants." Callie glanced over at me.

"Nah, crabby pants has to get back to work in a half hour," I replied.

"Oh, that sucks. Do you have to work a lot of split shifts?" Vincent asked curiously.

Callie and I both laughed.

"When doesn't she work?" Callie sighed gathering her stuff up. "Good luck with that."

"I work a good portion of the week. Usually, I'll take Wednesday and Thursday afternoon off to stay on top of school stuff. We're not open crazy late though, so it's not a huge deal," I replied to Vincent before glancing at Callie. "Have fun in potions!"

"If I survive this mid-semester exam I think it'll be okay." Callie sighed.

"Need my notes again?" I asked. I had already taken that class.

"If you don't mind." Callie's eyes lit up.

"Of course not. I've got class at eleven tomorrow. When's yours?" I asked as I typed a reminder into my phone.

"Ten thirty, that doesn't work. Can I swing by the shop before class?" Callie begged.

"Yeah, that works," I agreed and Callie headed out.

Vincent took her seat. "That's nice of you, crabby pants."

I rolled my eyes. "Of course I'll help with classes. The world needs a few less airheads."

"Agreed." He nodded.

"So, how'd that meeting whatever thing go?" I asked, not sure what else to say. "What brings an out of towner here, anyway?"

"Class stuff. Part of my major means I get the pleasure of helping out with classes around the nation," Vincent replied, already tired just from the thought.

"What major does that? Teaching?" I asked curiously.

"Leadership." He laughed.

"Ah, working on getting a palace job?" It wasn't uncommon for people to try that. Getting away from the small town life was exactly what I wanted to do, and what several old friends had gone off and done. We were only about three hours from the capital.

"You could say that." He smirked. "What about you? Majoring in anything fun?"

"Vague double major in Illusions and Potions with an undecided concentration in those fields. Mostly filling credits until I can afford to go to Queensland University," I explained.

"Oh, that's awesome. They're a really good school. What about scholarships?"

I shrugged. Why did everyone ask that? "I'm not able to get most since my family does have a good business, but my stepmother wants zero to do with me leaving. Of course, I'll try for the few I can, but even my luck brews aren't going to be enough to assure me a place there."

"Never know, I've had some great luck all around today. You might have some exceptional talent." Vincent offered a smile.

"While I'll accept that is totally my doing, I doubt it's exceptional. I just excel at potions and brewing some luck into coffee isn't more than a level two task. Good try, though."

"Come on, a little confidence," Vincent tried to urge me.

I gave a laugh and packed up my books. "I have every bit of confidence you'll be back for another coffee tomorrow and that Diamond will be all over you. Sorry, the luck doesn't last that long."

"That's not fair, that's some good coffee." He sighed dramatically.

"See ya tomorrow then." I waved and headed off.

The next morning Diamond came in wide awake and ready to go. Armed with the cute guy's name, which she and Rose had begged and begged my ear off for when we were closing shop last night, and some overly flirty clothes, they waited.

Unimpressed, I made quick work of the morning rush steaming latte after latte filled with various magical boosts. It seemed every student wanted to get in and get some luck or charm as they hoped to accidentally meet the visiting prince. The prince had apparently arrived yesterday or the day before in town. How could someone so important appear that covertly?

While Diamond may have been setting her sights on the new guy, that didn't stop her from flirting with any cute guy that came in. Some rolled with it, some fell for it, and one clueless guy didn't seem to get the hint. The only reason I knew Vincent came in was from the increased giggling and the loud use of his name. Diamond tried to play it off that she saw his name in a dream and to my surprise, he went with it. I wasn't sure if he was doing that to get through this conversation quicker or if he was actually amused by her attempt.

Either way, I tiredly handed him his latte.

"It's packed this morning. Is it normally this busy?" he asked, looking around and seeing no empty seats.

"Not unless it's finals week. I guess that prince Alexander is in town and visiting the school," I replied. Both Rose and Diamond had said his name enough yesterday that I knew I wasn't misremembering it.

"That must be exciting. I did hear he was doing a few events," Vincent agreed.

"Probably." I shrugged. "I'm sure it would be interesting to hear what he'd have to say, and I've heard nothing but great things about his magic abilities, but alas, I've got work."

"That sucks. Maybe he'll appear in one of your classes," Vincent replied, giving his new drink, vanilla cinnamon with a charisma boost, a tentative sip.

"I'm not going to get my hopes up. At least Callie's going to try and record the seminar for me. I'm actually really interested in hearing it." I smiled, shrugged, and since the line was finally done, went about getting things restocked before I had to rush off to class.

I barely skidded into class with a minute to spare when I noticed Vincent was there talking with the teacher. I raised an eyebrow at him as I took my seat. This wasn't a leadership things type class.

He gave a small wave as he continued to talk with the teacher. Shrugging, I got my things ready for class. I could freely pester him for real answers later.

The teacher finally cleared his throat and introduced Vincent to the room as class began. "All right, class. For our guest helper this week and next we have," He motioned vaguely in Vincent's direction. "Um, Vincent. He attended Queensland University and might have some great insight to share with the class."

For the most part, Vincent was just there and occasionally demonstrated some things. It was a fairly non active class. All questions asked from students and answers given to the teacher were from the same three people: me, Carissa, and Anthony.

Carissa, as bright and talented as she was, somehow happened to be Diamond's best friend. To no surprise, as soon as class was over, she was all over Vincent with a list of questions. I wouldn't be surprised if Diamond had snapped a picture of him and sent it to her. Poor guy. At least he only had a short time to deal with their nonsense. Eventually, he'd be done with this project and go back to wherever he had come from.

So, off to lunch I went. This semester was a dull one for me. I had one class a day, but they were fairly difficult classes. It always felt like I had a mound of homework, even if it was mostly practical application.

I was halfway through my chicken sandwich when Vincent found my table.

"I see you finally escaped Carissa," I teased.

"How is she friends with your step-sister?" He groaned, collapsing into the chair next to me. "She's clearly smart and talented."

"And extremely shallow." I snorted. The world had all kinds. "She has a very natural talent for illusion magic. This class might be the only thing she works at." I shrugged and took another bite of my sandwich before I remembered the question I wanted to ask him.

"I guess the world has all kinds." He sighed as he picked at his own lunch.

I finally finished chewing and was able to speak again. "I thought you were doing leadership stuff. What's up with being in my class?"

Vincent blushed and gave a nervous laugh. "I just really didn't feel like explaining why I was in town and at the school. It worked out well that you accepted my vague answer. Until now, of course."

"Vagueness accepted." I nodded. "Welcome to the non-judgement table." I took another bite of my burger.

"Just like that? No twenty questions?" He seemed skeptical.

I rolled my eyes and finished chewing faster. "You'll be gone in what, a week? As fun as twenty questions would be, I don't think knowing your favorite color will matter in a month."

"No long distance friendships for you, then? Just the continued role of crabby barista?" He smirked.

"My lovely step-sisters would be more than thrilled to destroy another friendship, even more so if it's with a guy they can't have." I shrugged, returning the focus to my meal.

"That sucks." He frowned. "Are they always so terrible to you?"

I shrugged and chewed at a normal rate before replying. "I wouldn't say they're awful, but they're pretty close to it. I get paid at least."

"How would they even destroy a friendship?"

"The short of it is they'll never leave you alone if you have any connection with me. Callie isn't a threat to them, so she's been around for a while. She's equally school focused and doesn't get me to take time off work, so they're fine with her."

"I can handle them," Vincent said with a confident smile.

"Uh huh." I shook my head. "Anyway, you'll be gone soon."

"I'll be here for another week after this one and then maybe for a week at the end of the semester," Vincent corrected. "So, let's try this friendship thing. If you win, you were right. No surprise to you. But if I'm right, you've got a friend. Come on, what's the worst that can happen?"

"Diamond sobbing that I'm talking to the man of her dreams." I rolled my eyes.

"You mean man of her week. She'll get over it." He laughed but there was no humor in his face.

I had to laugh. He was right. "Well, you've figured that out, but until someone she finds more attractive walks in, you're stuck."

"How does she ever get a date?" He sighed, stealing a fry from my plate.

I swatted his hand away. "Don't know. Don't care. She's dated maybe four guys this year? It's not like she's not known for being problematic."

"This year? It's March." Vincent seemed surprised.

"Thankfully, Rose has been going steady with someone for the last eight months. We'll see how that goes." I shrugged.

"And you?" He asked curiously.

"What part of they want to ruin everything don't you get?" I was a bit more annoyed than called for. Taking a breath, I tried to reply more calmly this time. "I dated one guy three years ago and they promised him the worst string of bad luck in the universe unless he broke up with me. He didn't believe them for about four days. It's not worth the effort until I can move away."

"That's rough." He frowned. "How can anyone be that terrible?"

"Don't know, but facts are facts." My phone beeped at me. "And I need to get back to work, so what else is new?"

"Can I get your number before you run off?" he asked. "It'll be easier to be long distance friends if we can chat."

I rolled my eyes. "Only if you explain what you're actually doing here."

"I thought this was the no judgement table." He laughed.

"The table is, the phone on the other hand, is not." I was pretty proud of my reply and couldn't help but smirk at him.

"It's a deal then." He offered his hand.

I shook it and summoned my magic to place an illusion on his hand. "There you have it. That should be easy enough for you to dispel."

He looked at it and nodded as he dug out his phone.

"Later then." I gathered my stuff together.

"Later." He smiled back at me.

CHAPTER 3

I didn't know why I was surprised to receive a message later that wasn't from Callie. It had almost slipped my mind that Vincent wanted my number. Whatever, I had warned him as best I could. At least at this point in time I had my own phone plan. While I hated having the additional expense, it was far better than the stepmother reading over every last detail of my phone history.

"How's it going?"

I stared at the simple message as I locked up the shop and headed upstairs. It was nice having the small flat to myself and made opening and closing easier. Not that I was far from my step-family. They were simply down the street, within reasonable walking distance at that.

"The usual." I had nothing to say. Instead, I pulled out my books and began reading the next assignment. It was focusing on detecting and dispelling illusions that were not on you personally – something I hated working on.

It was hard to work on illusions individually. If I cast a spell on an object, of course I'd be able to detect it. It was a completely different story trying to pick up on someone else's magic, and it all depended on how strong they were. If they were too far above my level I might never notice. Dispelling something stronger than you was nearly impossible.

My phone chimed again. *"That's not very descriptive."*

"Ah, my mistake." I rolled my eyes and took a picture of my book. *"Instead of work work, it's onto school work."*

"Exciting," came his response.

"It would be if I could break through anyone's illusions. Now that would be fun stuff." No lie there. I could easily have my scholarship then.

"Just takes time. You've got the dedication for it."

"Dedication only goes so far. You need massive talent for that." I wasn't afraid to keep trying, but eventually everyone's skills topped out somewhere.

"You're right, you need practice."

I wasn't sure how to respond to that. He wasn't wrong. "Very true. I'm sure we'll be doing more actual applications in class again instead of discussing theory since the upcoming section is more hands on."

"That is what your teacher, Mr. Whittaker I think his name was, is planning, but you need more practice outside of class. Do they have a place around here where you can actually do that? Rooms with items to detect spells and figure out what it is and work on breaking them?"

City boy had no idea. I shook my head at my phone. "Nope. Nothing too fancy here. Either you move on to a bigger school or get stuck around here."

"Geez, where is the school funding going if it's magic department is so lacking?" I could almost hear the disappointment in his message.

"*Welcome to forgotten county schools. Where the classes exist but nothing more than that!*" It was painfully true.

"*Yeah, I'm starting to notice that. Bring a few books tomorrow and I'll put some spells on them. Sure, you'll know they have spells on them, but at least you can work on figuring out which ones exactly. Some help is better than none.*"

I was surprised by his message. "*Thanks, I appreciate the help.*"

"*Of course. Who wouldn't help with school work? ;)*"

Oooh, my own words against me. Clever boy. Maybe I was wrong. This could be a decent friendship if he actually wanted to help. I hated to think of what my family might do about it, though. At least he'd be away soon enough so it wouldn't matter.

Work went much the same the next day. Wednesday was normally our slowest day, but this prince stuff had people wanting a little extra magic in their lives – just in case. I couldn't blame them. It was probably the most interesting event in town since the time someone had let eight chickens and five lobsters loose in the grocery store. Even that had been several years ago.

The line seemed to reach out the door forever and it was nearly time for me to head to class when I finally saw there were only three people left. Poor Vincent was the last one and Diamond made sure she had a chance to talk his ear off. I set his drink on the pickup counter but Diamond seemed to have him caught up in a story.

Oh well, he'd have to figure a way out himself.

Quickly, I vanished into the back. "Steph, time for class!"

Steph yawned at me. "Already? Geez. I'll get on bar then. Good luck!"

I tossed my apron in the bin and tried to put on my coat as I grabbed my bag. "Thanks! Going to need it with how busy campus has been."

"Maybe you'll meet the prince." Steph giggled.

"Sure, I'd likely run straight into him, apologize, and head off to class and not realize it for several hours." I laughed back, finally getting everything on right. Truthfully, I wouldn't even know hours later. I had zero clue what he looked like. I should look up a picture if I ever remembered in my spare time.

"That would be you," she agreed, heading out front with me.

I took note that Vincent had managed to get his drink but that hadn't stopped Diamond from continuing the conversation over at the pickup counter.

"Good luck," I said to Steph and rushed off.

It had gotten colder outside than I expected and I said a silent prayer that my rust bucket of a car would start. Okay, it actually looked pretty decent on the outside, but it was a fifteen-year-old car and had a lot of issues on the inside. So, of course, it wouldn't start. Early spring weather was going to be the death of me. Try as I might to get it to turn over, nothing happened when I turned the key. I groaned loudly and rested my head on the wheel. I should have given myself a luck boost this morning but no, I had to go with the energy one. Great choice, past self. Great choice.

Well, I hadn't missed a day yet this semester so it wasn't a huge deal, but still. I hated missing class. Even more so if we were actually doing practical application. The theory stuff I could always read in my free time, but application was so much harder when you were outside of class.

A knock on my window startled me

I looked over to see Vincent standing there with a concerned look. I opened my door.

"You okay?" He asked.

"Yeah, my car won't start." I sighed.

"Does it just need a jump, or is something else wrong?"

"Hopefully just a jump, but I've no idea," I admitted.

"Well, I've got jumpers, so let's try that," he said, going back over to his car.

Not having time to argue against the help, I popped open the hood.

"I actually don't know how to use them, though," he admitted, handing them to me.

I gave a small laugh and went about setting it up. "Sadly this isn't the first time I've had to do this. So, either a jump will work or the battery is dead." How many times did I jump it last year? How old was the battery anyway? I couldn't remember, so it was prob-ably old enough to be dead. "Go start your car," I instructed. After a few moments, I tried mine and nothing happened. Nothing again.

"It's not working?" The disappointment in his voice mirrored how I felt.

"Pretty much. Now you're late for no reason." At least he had offered to help. "Guess I'll just miss today and figure out how to get a new battery."

"Or I could give you a ride?" He laughed, shaking his head at me.

Oh. That hadn't occurred to me. "Yeah, that would make sense." I grabbed my bag and got him his cables back. "Thanks," I said as we finally headed off toward the school. "Sorry you're late, though."

"It happens." He shrugged not seeming to mind. "I'm sure everyone will understand winter car problems."

It dawned on me that Diamond might have seen me leave with Vincent. "Shoot, I hope my sister doesn't notice."

"Think she'd really hate you for needing a ride?"

"If you didn't pick up on the not caring for my existence, let alone me talking with the current man of her dreams, then I'd be surprised if she was cool with it," I replied dryly.

"She is certainly dreaming on that one." He snorted, disgust evident on his face.

"So, what's your dream girl then if it's not some shallow illusion?" I asked, amused by his reaction.

Vincent shrugged, not taking his eyes off the road. "I don't know. I guess similar interests, a fun personality? Ummm... probably with some sort of magical talent. Magic users tend to have a better understanding of one another. I don't know."

"How wonderfully generic." I laughed.

"Fine, what's your dream guy then?" He smirked as I fumbled to find an answer.

"Uhhh...." I had to laugh. "You've got me. I'll go with generic ideal soulmate excuse for the win. Though I'll throw in they need to have a decent taste in music."

"Ohhh generic with a subjective viewpoint. What is decent taste in music then?" he asked pulling into the parking lot.

"We can swap lists later. I've got a sprint ahead of me," I replied. "But thanks so much for the ride."

"Any time," he replied, giving me a friendly wave.

After class, Callie was on me about why I had been late. I was always at least somewhat early.

"Wait, Vincent gave you a ride? That's awesome luck." Callie seemed a bit too excited about it.

"Good luck that he was there, yes, but now I need to find a ride to get a battery and that's more money out of my savings." I gently hit my head against the table a few times before looking up at Callie.

"True. That car hasn't helped with your savings plan at all this year." Callie sighed but quickly smiled. "Still, cute boy gave you a ride."

"Cute boy that my crazy step sister has her eyes on." I sat up straight. "I really don't want her drama in my life."

"Ah…" Callie relented. "True. Darn. It'd be so cool for you to finally have a date."

"We both know full well I can go on dates. Just with their approved list." I cringed as a shiver worked its way through me. Their list was… less than appealing.

"Ew. Have they made any more recommendations on that end?" Callie cringed with me.

"Evan Baxter." I gave her the most disgusted look I could manage. My stomach turned at the thought of my sister trying to hook me up with her favorite hookup. There were too many levels of wrong there.

"Your sister's on again off again thing? How is that even a suggestion?" The grossed out look covered all my feelings on the subject.

"I'm assuming because my sister doesn't actually want him but he'd be a good family connection. His family is worth quite a bit." I tried to shake the thought of him near me from my head. "I don't know why we pretend to be in modern ages when they literally want to marry me off for social ties."

"Because they suck." Callie shook her head before spotting Vincent and waving him over.

Vincent joined us with his tray of food. "Afternoon, ladies."

"There's the man of the hour." Callie laughed. "Great job on the rescue mission."

Vincent shrugged. "We were going to the same place. Of course I'd help?" He seemed confused by her excitement.

I shook my head. "Callie thinks this is over the top exciting news."

"You talking to anyone new kind of is," she pointed out.

"Yes, every three years or so I swap out friends. Guess this is the beginning of that rotation," I teased.

"You can't get rid of me. We'll both be stuck here forever," Callie joked back.

"Ugh, don't hold me down here," I grumbled as I poked at my lunch.

"I won't. That car will, though." Callie smirked. "How much has it cost you this year?"

"Too much," I agreed, "but whatever. It is what it is."

"If you can hang around until my next class is over I can take you to get a battery." Callie glanced at her watch before taking a giant bite of her food.

"Yeah, I'll just have to call the store and let them know. Not like any of them want to or can pick me up."

Callie glanced over at Vincent. "Unless you're free sooner?"

Vincent shook his head. "I've got two classes after this," he admitted.

"Well, let's see who answers the phone. If it's Diamond she'll demand details. If it's Steph, she'll be whatever," I said pulling out my phone.

"What if it's your stepmom?" Callie leaned closer, as if she could hear the person on the other line. "Lecture?"

"Of course. Lectures are her favorite thing. Clearly, I'm terribly irresponsible. I let this happen."

"They all die eventually." Callie shrugged.

The phone rang twice before Diamond picked up. Sighing, I explained that my car was dead and that I'd be late getting back because I needed to wait on a ride. To my surprise, she just wanted to know details I picked up from Vincent. She saw us leave together and she hoped I knew better than to try and steal her man.

I glanced over at Callie and Vincent and rolled my eyes. "Of course, I'm not stealing your man. You've got a chance. He loves a girl with magic. Sadly, I did find out he's only here another week before continuing his school rotation thing."

"What?" She screamed into the phone. "He can't leave!"

"It's a sad truth. He'll be gone soon. Maybe you can make long distance work," I suggested, rolling my eyes once again as Callie tried to stifle a laugh. Vincent looked annoyed at the thought.

"Forget that. I'll get what I want from him then be done." With that she hung up on me and I laughed.

"What was that?" Callie asked, already laughing.

"I don't know if I want to know." Vincent eyed me carefully.

"She won't do long distance, so good for you Vincent." I glanced over at Callie who was stifling a giggle.

"But?" He knew something was coming.

"She'll get what she wants before you leave." I tried to stifle a laugh as well. "Good luck dealing with her now."

"What is wrong with her?" He groaned tiredly. He raked his hands through his hair as he vaguely motioned for a moment before giving up on speaking and just shook his head.

"I don't have time to write a list." I shrugged, going back to my lunch.

"The funny thing is she's not as bad as she used to be." Callie glanced at her watch again. "Well, this has been fun but I've got class."

Nodding, I continued eating my lunch as she left.

Vincent sighed. "I think I just might avoid the shop, then."

"I wouldn't blame you." I felt a little disappointed. Why did I feel that way? He was gone soon anyway.

"Unless you want me to stop by." He seemed to be watching my face carefully.

"I wouldn't put anyone through that hell." I shook my head. Everyone deserved better.

We were quiet for a moment before he spoke again. "Oh! Did you bring those extra books?" He seemed happy to remember last night's offer.

"Oh yeah, I completely forgot about that." I pulled a few from my bag. "Thanks again."

"No problem. I hope the school can get its programs together. There isn't much room for continued success past the basics of the programs." He took the first book and quietly muttered something.

"It probably won't. It's not uncommon for small local colleges to have just the basics. You worry too much about something that's not going to change." I continued eating my lunch.

Vincent quickly worked his way through the small stack before handing them back. "You don't know what can't change until you try." He gave a wink. "Anyway, bring them back tomorrow and I can do that again."

"Sure." I shrugged. "I'll try, anyway. I hate figuring out how to detect and dispel illusions. What's the point if it's not bothering me?"

"There're several good points. Seeing someone for their true self. You can learn how to see past illusions without dispelling them. That even works on places. It's extremely helpful."

"Maybe in places with a high mage population. It's fairly underdeveloped skill sets here."

"True as that might be, if you really want out of here, wouldn't that be perfect to know?" He smirked, knowing he had won.

"Fine. You've got this round." I shook my head and put the books away.

"I intend to win them all." He gave a sly smile.

"Like what? Best music, because you haven't listed a single song. A loss in itself," I replied smugly.

"Now sadly, I have to get to class, but, I will have a list for you and another win for me," he replied, gathering up his things.

"Uh huh." I rolled my eyes at him.

"What about video games and books?" he asked as he slung his bag over his shoulder.

"I haven't played too many games recently. Just not a lot of extra funds. Ebooks have saved me a ton though," I replied.

"Top five trade off later?" he asked, not moving until I gave my answer.

"Sure. Top five. Three topics. Be ready to defend your choices," I agreed. With a smile, he waved and headed off.

I certainly planned to challenge his list and started to mentally prep mine. Wait, was that flirting? I shook my head before it hit me that I was going to miss him when he left. Ugh, stupid boy feelings.

CHAPTER 4

It was getting late when Vincent messaged me. Late for me anyway. Being up at four in the morning kind of ruined what was left of my social life.

"Top five music?"

I shook my head at the question. *"Nope, you have to answer first. That was my question."*

"That's not fair. Not fair for you since you'll have to answer mine first then!" Without hesitating, he listed his favorite bands and four of the five were mine.

"Trade Total Temptation for Deathwish and you have a real list." I couldn't help but laugh.

"*Nah, that's an easy top 10, but we're only doing the absolute bests.*"

I raised an eyebrow at the message. "*Those are fighting words right there.*"

"*Bring it.*" he sent back.

Laughing, I didn't know what to say. Anything that came to mind came off as flirty. Was this whole thing flirty? I was out of my element here.

"*Top five games?*"

Back and forth, we bantered about our favorites until I finally had to call it quits.

"*Gotta sleep. Work's too early not to.*"

"*Ah, that sucks. Okay.*" There was a pause before he sent, "*Oh did you finish dispelling all that stuff?*"

"*If I say yes can we pretend it's true? It's a lot harder than I was expecting.*" I hated admitting I couldn't get them all, let alone only being able to knock out one.

"*Haha, no. It's no big deal. You just need more work. Didn't you say something about time off of work? I can help you.*"

I shook my head. I forgot I had told him that. "*Normally yes, but my youngest step-sister had a 'big project' this week so I was working her hours. So, no off day for me."*

"What about after work?"

"I don't know." This was hard. I didn't want to deal with Diamond finding out about this friendship, but I also did need help.

"Secret meet up? All covert and hush hush?"

"Fine. Meet at close. Bring the magic." I gave in. We'd have to see how this went.

"Excellent. Mission magic meetup has been accepted. Until then!"

Until then indeed.

The day went by quickly. Diamond was upset in the morning when Vincent didn't show up. I shrugged it off, suggesting he might be sick. The terrible weather could do that to anyone. I just didn't mention he was at school. Diamond skipped out of work early, leaving just Steph and I to close. No big deal. We put on some good closing music and started to clean the floors for the last half hour. We'd barely get a handful of customers so late, and most wouldn't even notice the change in music.

In the last five minutes, Vincent came in as Steph was about to head out.

"Want me to jump on bar?" She was already bundled up and ready to go as I finished mopping the cafe area.

"Nah, go on." I waved her off.

Steph shrugged before heading out the door. "Until dawn!"

"May your dreams not be of here." I called back as I laughed at her dramatic exit.

"Looks like I picked just the right time." Vincent grabbed a seat.

"That is does." I gathered up the mop and whatnot cleaning supplies. "Want a drink?"

"Do you have any teas?"

"Sure, what kind? We've got all the basics covered." I walked around the counter towards the tea.

"Something herbal and sweet."

"Always with the sweet." I sighed trying to guess which would be the best.

"Of course. I'm not a bitter person." He smiled brightly.

"Uh huh." I prepped the tea. "Where would you like to go practice? I'd really hate for Diamond to see your car here."

"Hm? Oh." He glanced back at his car and muttered something for a few moments and it was gone. "Next problem?"

"I suppose I shouldn't be surprised the illusion guy could hide a car." I laughed, leaning on the counter.

"Objects are the easiest to manipulate. Living things are a little more complicated." He shrugged.

"True." I brought his tea over. "Guess I'll go grab the books."

"I'm surprised you're not worried about her driving by and seeing someone in here." Vincent smirked.

"I'm surprised the illusion master didn't notice you can't see from the outside in." I raised an eyebrow and happily walked off. I could hear him mutter 'Well, now I do' as I left.

My bag was just sitting in the back so it was a quick trip.

"That spell is pretty decent. Did you do it?" He asked curiously.

I shook my head. "Carissa, Diamond's friend, did that like two years ago. She's crazy talented. It's just starting to wear down, but it'll probably last several more months."

He looked to be deep thought for a moment as he nodded to himself. "There are some great layers to it. She has a tutor, right?"

"I believe so." I shrugged. "Wouldn't surprise me."

"You can do better than this spell by Sunday," he stated, catching me off guard.

"Psh, no." I laughed, taking the seat across from him.

"Sure, I could be wrong. But what if I'm right?" He raised an eyebrow. "Now, which one did you figure out?" He motioned toward my bag.

I started pulling everything out and he quickly jumped into a lesson – going through the varying layers of the different magics and how they could strengthen one another. Finding the fringes of where these magics met reality was the biggest part of detecting an illusion.

Slowly we worked through getting through the spells he placed on the books and what went into each one.

Finally, I couldn't stop yawning. "We're going to have to call it a night."

Vincent nodded, echoing my yawn. "At least you got some of this down better."

I nodded, feeling more tired than happy about it.

"Most of the stronger mages have three areas they excel at and concentrate their studies in," he stated offhandedly.

"Mhm. And did you want to brag about yours?" I gave a small laugh as I took his cup back to be washed.

"Well, I suppose I could. You already know my best one, then there's enchanting and destruction."

"Fancy. If you can't fool them, destroy them." I smirked.

"Haha." He rolled his eyes at me. "What about you? I'd love to know how your magic works together."

"Eh, I've just concentrated on the two. It's too expensive to worry about a third. Illusion is a lot of work as it is, but I've a natural enough talent for potions and mixtures." I shrugged, setting the cup into the sink.

"But what is the third? I knew you had one," he happily pressed on.

I rolled my eyes but conjured up an orb of light. I left it to hang above the sink.

"That's pretty awesome." He actually seemed impressed.

"It's just a light." I shrugged. It was one of the easiest spells to learn in the conjuration class.

"You should consider it. There was no hesitation in creating that," he insisted.

"I've no idea how to make you understand it's just not possible right now." I sighed, coming back around to gather up my books.

"I'll think on it," he said finally as he stood up. "Tomorrow, then?"

I had no idea what there was to think on. There was no easy way to turn everything around and just make it work. I shrugged. "Sure. Unless you would rather do something else. This can't be too exciting."

"Proving you wrong will be exciting enough." He wasn't going to give up on that 'by Sunday' idea. "I will help you improve this. Though I'll have to leave some extra hard assignments behind when I leave. No way you can slack off once you've made progress." His friendly smile turned to a sly smirk.

"Uh huh, just keep telling yourself that." I unlocked the door to let him out.

"I will." With that, he left.

Silly know-it-all boys. Quickly, I locked the door and gathered up my books. It was getting to be past my bedtime.

CHAPTER 5

Friday went much the same. Saturday did as well, minus the whole no school part. Vincent arrived just before close and I was stuck thinking up a plan to counter today's nuttiness. He instantly noticed my frown.

"Something wrong?" He asked, confused.

"So, Diamond and Rose are having some friends by for a scrapbooking get together in about an hour. They'll pretty much make a mess of everything I just cleaned, but that's beside the point. I've no idea where to move practice. Too many places will be closed in about an hour." I sighed.

Vincent frowned. "Oh, that sucks. I don't want to cause more drama. I don't think you'd enjoy practicing in my small hotel room either."

"No…" But it gave me an idea. "I do have the loft upstairs. At least there's a somewhat living room. Really, it's all one giant room. Slightly less weird, but still weird. Couldn't you have come in the fall when it's nice out?"

He laughed. "I was around the other half of the country then. It's been a busy year of travel."

"Do you miss home?" I asked curiously.

"Here and there. It's been fun meeting a lot of people. A couple of locations were rather flat on that end, but whatever." He shrugged.

"That sucks." I noticed Diamond pull in. "Hey, my sister's here. So, either you can sneak out the back or come upstairs."

"Do you want to practice? I'm leaving this choice to you," he asked.

I really did. It actually felt like I was getting somewhere. "Fine, let's go." I quickly lead him around the back and up the stairs.

My little flat didn't have much to offer, but it would work fine for practice. "Ignore the mess," I stated as I glanced around. My laundry basket was full to the brim, the bed unmade, and I had a few assignments spread across the coffee table and half the floor. At least I knew the bathroom was clean, though there were probably far too many lotions out. There were worse problems in life.

"This is hardly a mess." He laughed.

Shrugging, I motioned for him to sit while I gathered up the assignments into one pile. "Better than normal." I turned to face him. "So, what's today's lesson?"

"How about a fun game? I'll change several things around here and you change them back. I won't say what or how many. I just need a moment." He glanced around from his seat. "Though it may not be too hard with the minimalist vibe you've got going."

"There were a few fun posters before I moved here. Diamond destroyed those. Rose smashed up some things too." I considered the several things I had lost over the years to them. "Eh, whatever." I tried to shrug it off.

"Your family is too abusive," he stated the obvious softly.

"Too late to change things now. Anyway, aren't we going to work on magic things? Who needs a weekend sob story?" I sat on the floor across from him. He seemed to get the hint and changed topics back to magic.

"Sure. Close your eyes." He waited for me to follow along with the directions before I felt his magic actively working. After several different mutterings that he made too hard to hear, he was ready. "All right, have at it."

The minimalist part made seeing the differences for some things easy. I knew my table wasn't that long, and I knew my curtains were a darker gray. It looked like my cup was out of place, but I ignored the obvious facts and instead concentrated on feeling the magic out. The easiest one that came to me was actually my bag slumped over on the floor. Visually, I had hardly noticed a difference in it.

Untangling the threads and dispelling the effects on it took seconds. That made me proud, but I tried not to get caught up on it. Instead I moved onto the next thing and slowly untangled everything I could.

"I think I got them all..." I stated after awhile. I could already feel a slight strain on my magic. Still, I couldn't help but smile that it had taken me less than twenty minutes.

"That you did," Vincent agreed with a smile of his own.

That only encouraged me to smirk. "Guess that wasn't too bad at all."

"See? I know you could totally take down Carissa's illusion now if you wanted to."

I couldn't argue with him. I could feel it, the illusion that had hung around for so long wasn't beyond me right now. Rebuilding it would be a different story. "But I couldn't cast one like it."

"I think you could cast a better one, though I understand your reluctance. It is hard. You need to know exactly how you want things to look for the observers. There can be zero hesitating when casting the spell and zero doubt in your mind to make it work better than hers." He let the facts hang in the air for a moment before continuing. "I've no reason to waste my time with lies though. I think you're better than her. You've just had less time and tools to build your skills and confidence."

There was no reason to doubt him. He really had nothing to gain by helping out. It was a means to pass time maybe, but that didn't give him a reason to lie.

"Maybe," I relented a little.

"I'd like you to try casting a strong illusion charm. Let's see how strong you can make one." He gave me an encouraging smile.

I closed my eyes. I hated trying to remember all the various sayings and incantations that went with illusions. I prefered to cut them down however I could. The less to remember saying the better.

He wanted a strong illusion charm? Fine. I opened my eyes and smirked at him.

"All right teach, close your eyes, I think I've got an idea." This could be fun.

"By all means." He leaned back and closed his eyes.

I knew exactly what I wanted to do. Happily, I closed my eyes once more and let my magic grip onto the sofa and the area rug below it. I wanted it to look exactly like a cloudy sky, and upon seeing it, give the feeling of falling. My brain searched for the right keywords that were needed and I mumbled the shortened spell as I put the visualization into magic.

When I opened my eyes, it was done. A little too well. I felt the overwhelming fear of falling and had to look up. "Okay, all your problem now." I laughed toward the ceiling.

He saw me looking up and looked up too, confused. Seeing nothing he felt with his magic what was amiss and looked down. "Why a falling illusion?" He groaned and looked up again.

"Because they're annoying and fun all at once." I laughed evilly. Maybe with a tad too much glee.

"Very true, and annoying to break." He closed his eyes in turn and after a few short moments it was gone. "You mumbled maybe six words. How did you even do all of that?"

I shrugged. "I hate long spells." It was the truth.

"And you don't believe you are good at this?" He laughed. "Most people can't shorten spells, and here you did an illusion with full effects."

"It can't be that uncommon. Sure, maybe here, but you've seen the schooling. It's not exactly amazing." No need to talk something up that wasn't grand.

"As someone who has actually been all over this year I can say that." He shook his head. "You just need the right teachers."

It was weird hearing I was uncommonly good at something. Maybe I was wrong. Unlikely though.

"At this point, it's just practice and refining." Vincent went on after a moment of silence. "I've no doubt you'll be able to do exactly what I've already been doing without issue if you just keep this up." He laughed. "Seriously, I'm going to get back and you might even be my equal."

"Why would you come back?" I asked, shaking my head. "This school probably doesn't have much to offer you, whatever it is you're doing."

"Because I decided to. I had a little freedom with the last bit of traveling." He shrugged.

I stared at him, confused. "Again, why? No one wants to come back here. Most people would rather leave."

"Because my new bestie is here, and I want to help her succeed." He shrugged and offered me a smile.

I had no idea what to say. "Come on, you'll find somewhere better to revisit."

"There are more interesting places, yes. My statement still stands."

I couldn't think of anything better to say. So, I just shrugged.

"So, since that's a victory for me, do you want to practice more or do you have another idea?" Vincent asked.

"This town is no victory, but I appreciate the help. There is still plenty of time to change your mind." I shook my head. "That last spell was actually a bit more tiring than I should have done. So, I can offer old video games from my ten-year-old console and some mini pizzas. Or we can have fun sneaking you out."

"How long are they going to be here do you think?" He asked curiously.

"More than several rounds of me kicking your butt in Smash Karts." I smirked.

"Well, that decides it. You're on. I always win."

Laughing, I got up and turned it on. I turned to give him a sweet smile before clicking my tongue at him. "Used to always win."

For once, he was wrong.

Sunday was my sleep-in day. Or it was supposed to be. We were closed, but from the constant chime of my phone, it seemed someone hadn't gotten the memo. I glanced at the screen to see several missed texts from Vincent. Something about wanting to know if I wanted to do anything today since I was off.

"Don't you ever sleep?" I messaged back and buried my face in the pillow.

My phone decided to not chime its text alert this time but ring instead. The normally hilarious sound of a voice saying 'ring ring' instead was annoying. Sighing, I gave in and answered.

"Mhm?" I mumbled into the phone.

"I thought it was normal to start with hello," Vincent replied, his voice sounding too amused.

"'S early. Can't I sleep in?" I grumbled back.

"Nine isn't that early," Vincent replied, no less amused.

"Uh huh," I mumbled back.

"Aside from sleeping, did you have any plans today?" Vincent pressed on.

"I don't know. Maybe watch some old movies. Maybe tackle some laundry. I don't know… why?" I yawned. There was no chance of going back to sleep now, though.

"What about brunch? My treat," he asked. I could hear the hesitation in his voice.

I wasn't sure how to take the offer. "I should probably get things done today," I replied hesitantly.

"I'm sure you've got to eat sometime." Oooh, good counter.

"I live off of the hopes and dreams of every person that comes to the door forgetting we are closed Sunday." It was actually a very amusing sight.

"So, does that mean you don't like pancakes?"

"Pancakes are great, but have you tried french toast casserole? Wait, you're not from here. Ugh, fine, I'm up." I finally sat up and rubbed the sand from my eyes.

"I don't think I've heard of such a thing," Vincent admitted.

"Inconceivable. Give me twenty to get ready. We're going to have to show you probably the only good thing that's come out of this small town."

Vincent chuckled. "It can't be that good."

"Psh, you've no idea. I'd even recommend this to the prince. It's that ungodly good."

"Oh, would you now?" He seemed extra amused by the idea.

"Nah, probably not." I laughed. "I was telling Steph with my luck I'd run into him and give a half-hearted apology before continuing on and not realise until several hours later it was him. Now that's much more accurate."

"You're the only person in town not obsessed with meeting him."

I shrugged, not that he could see it. "Meh, probably not. You don't seem that excited, and Callie's interest is more on what he could be doing out here than anything else. I think Steph isn't that excited either."

"Well, of course I'm not. I've met him."

"Really?" That was an interesting statement. "Is he an interesting person or not worth the hype?"

"Somewhere in between. Fairly interesting person. Mildly down to earth. Guess you can't ask much more from someone who's handed nearly everything in life."

"You're probably right. Guess I can go back to being uninterested now that I know all there is to know." I laughed.

"You see, this is why I'm voting you the least interested. Anyone else would have wanted to known how I met him, when this was, where we talked, and a hundred other details."

"As exciting as those details would be, it's not going to help me get french toast casserole and I'm never going to have any interactions with the guy, save for the likelihood of running into him head on while on my way to class." I shook my head and forced myself to find some clean clothes. "Besides, I'm sure even the prince would like to have some privacy in his life. Everyone doesn't need the details about everything."

"So, if you were given a chance to ask him anything you wouldn't?" Vincent mused.

"Not saying that," I started to shuffle through the clothes that had fallen out of my hamper onto the floor. "He's got a lot of magical talent. There's plenty to ask that isn't intrusive and that could be potentially enlightening for someone who is trying to better their abilities. Oh, I do have matching socks!" I found myself sidetracked by my hunt for clothes.

Vincent just laughed. "I'll pick you up in twenty then. Good luck with your socks."

"The luck has been had!" I laughed. "See ya then." Quickly I ended the call and hopped in the shower. Twenty minutes? Who was I kidding? I didn't normally move that fast.

Still I tried, and failed.

I glanced at my phone as I hopped out of the shower and saw that twenty-three minutes had passed. Of course they had. Showers were portals that stole your time in exchange for a brief moment of the perfect temperature of hot water.

Frantically I sent a text. "*I apologize in advance for who I am as a person.*" And continued getting ready.

It didn't take long to chime back at me. "*I'm not sure what that means.*"

I had to laugh. "*Running late. I do not do this morning person thing well.*"

"*Sure had me fooled,*" he quickly replied.

"*You've only seen me after several cups of coffee. You've gotten off easy until now.*"

"*Forgive me for not being scared. I'm sure no coffee mode isn't that terrible.*"

I glanced down at my worst pair of jeans, worst because they were covered in random paint stains, and the baggy hoodie I was wearing. No coffee mode meant no will to dress nicely. Though, for the sake of being out and about I willed my magic to make my pants look more normal. Illusion magic was the best gift I could ask for.

Calling it good enough, I braided my wet hair as I went downstairs and headed out. Vincent glanced over as got in.

"That's not a terrible grumpy anti-morning person look," Vincent commented. "Though it took me a moment to realize you had magic on your pants." I had almost forgotten that with my magic being below his that he could easily see past the illusion without dispelling it.

"They're the comfiest pants ever, but sadly probably not the best for wearing out." I shrugged.

"How did you get so much paint on them?" he asked curiously.

"Secrets." I smirked. "Now onward to breakfast!"

Vincent looked like he was going to argue but instead backed out of the parking spot. "Okay, where to?"

I gave the directions and off we went. It wasn't too far away. Nothing was really far away in a small town, though. Both convenient and problematic. It made it so much harder to feel like you could get away from life for a bit.

As we got seated Vincent asked again, "Since we're apparently getting french toast casserole, we've got plenty of time to hear the story about why your pants have so much paint on them."

I had to laugh. Instead of answering, I pulled out my phone and pulled up some photos before handing it to him. "You can swipe through that album."

"Oh, I didn't know you painted," he said with more interest than I was expecting.

"I used to a lot." I shrugged.

"Why not anymore?" He glanced up from my phone.

I just shrugged.

Vincent frowned. "Most of these are really good. Why'd you give it up?"

"All of those don't exist anymore. Maybe I'll pick it up again someday in the future. Not worth the cost of supplies just to have them destroyed." I had said it so many times to Callie that I almost believed myself now.

Vincent didn't seem to know what to say. Instead, he went back to staring at the pictures on my phone. I knew there weren't too many in that album so he had to be flipping through the same ones while he thought.

"Nothing to get hung up about anymore. It sucks, it's over. Got plenty of bigger goals to conquer. Once I figure all this school stuff out I'm sure there'll be time to pick up hobbies again."

"I'm glad you're able to be positive about it. I bet you'd be able to do a lot of awesome art if you picked it up again."

I laughed. "And bins full of terrible art. Anyway, the secret of the pants has been revealed. Let's move on to different topics. Surely you've got a hobby outside of losing to Smash Karts?"

"Hey, I'm just rusty. I will beat you eventually." He rolled his eyes.

"You've got a week and no system of your own to practice on. Looks like victory is not in your favor." I was too amused by his claim. "So, what else do you do in your spare time?"

"I like archery and, if you can believe it, origami," Vincent replied.

The waitress came over and took our orders before I could comment. I was glad it was Hazel and not Carol, who I knew would have had at least a dozen questions for me. Honestly, Hazel probably did too. I normally came in here alone, maybe with Callie. Never with a guy. Even better, one they didn't know. Hazel would be keeping a close eye on us for sure. What better thing to do in a small town than people watch?

Vincent took note of how closely I was watching her. "Afraid she'll say something to your sister?"

"Oh, no, she wouldn't. Half the other staff would, but Diamond would have to run into them. I've no idea how she'd react. I didn't really think this idea through," I admitted.

"She'll have to get over it eventually. You're allowed to have friends." Vincent crossed his arms and leaned back in his seat.

"Ha, we'll see. I think she holds grudges longer than anything. You'll be safe in a little less than a week. No worries." I shrugged.

"I'm not afraid of her. Though I am almost curious as to what her new angle will be to try and get me to talk to her. She's obviously getting desperate and I'm not sure how bad it'll get."

"I don't even want that answer." I shook my head. "Tell you what. If you really want a coffee, I can bring you one on my way to class. That's probably a better idea than suffering through Di's nonsense."

"That's not fair to you though," Vincent replied. "I know you have to go straight to class and work doesn't really give you much in between time."

"Eh, it's not that big of a deal, though you're right about me not having much time." I sighed. It was a good idea. Just not the easiest to implement.

"I've got an idea." Vincent gave a wicked smile.

"Oh? Let's hear it then?" I leaned forward and rested my chin on my hand.

"How about a little magic game? I'll go with a different illusion and you can try and figure out which customer was me. With all the traffic you've had recently, you won't have much time, but it's still good practice."

I groaned. "And my least favorite thing to practice." I sighed and sat up straighter. "Fine. It's worth a shot, I guess. Can't hurt to try."

"See? It works out both parts of the problem. No Diamond pestering me, and you get better magic practice."

"Why didn't you just do that in the first place anyway? There's no way she didn't annoy you after day two." It was a great idea, and surprising that two illusionists didn't think of it sooner.

"Didn't think about it, honestly." Vincent shrugged.

"Fair enough."

With that, food had finally made its way out to our table.

We ate quickly, conversation a bit hard with such a deliciously distracting meal. I happily took the win for what it was. As much as I hated where I lived, there was no better cooking than a small town break-fast.

"So, what now?" he asked as we got back into the car.

"I should probably get some things done." My laundry pile screamed of nightmares. At least my dishes were minimal.

"That's fair. Thanks for coming out with me." He flashed me a smile before starting the car and heading out.

Darn him. Why did I want to hang out still? Whatever. He'd be gone in a week. Some time couldn't hurt, right? "Unless you're up for my movie marathon. Though, I still have to get laundry done." I made the suggestion while looking out the window. Why was it embarrassing to suggest? This boy had butterflies exploding in my stomach.

"That could be fun, if you don't mind the company." I had no doubt from his tone he was smirking, but still, it was safer to look out the window.

I didn't mind. Not at all. I don't know why that was causing me to blush. I did not want to think about a possible crush on this cute boy who would be skipping town shortly. Instead, I kept my focus on the nothing exciting out the window. Great game plan. "Not at all." There we go. I could still totally respond to things like a normal person.

Vincent chuckled. "So, what movie were you thinking?"

I thought for a moment. "I think next on the list is Cinderella. Not the animated one, the R&H version." I glanced at him.

"I don't know if I know which one you're referring to."

"One with more musical numbers and less talking animals." I was finally able to smile gleefully at him.

"Yeah, I've no idea which one you're talking about, but I can't say I've seen more than the standard musicals." Vincent shrugged.

I shook my head. "There is not enough time between now and next weekend to catch you up on everything you're missing."

He laughed. "I guess you'll just have to pick the best ones."

"I don't think there's even enough time for those…" I sighed dramatically. "What have you even been doing with your spare time?"

"Running around completing as many side quests as possible before continuing on with the main story?" He offered a shrug before laughing.

"Fair enough. This side quest probably won't advance any plot, but it'll be fun." We were finally back.

"If you insist." Vincent sounded more amused than anything else.

"I do." I nodded confidently. "Life would be unbearable without good movies. Adding a catchy tune to them just makes it all the better."

"Uh huh." Vincent shook his head.

"Come on." I grabbed his hand and pulled him across the parking lot. "It'll be fun."

He just laughed and followed along.

CHAPTER 6

Upstairs, I apologized for the mess and went to find the movie I was thinking of. I didn't have a stand for them, so they lived in a box instead. When I turned around I saw Vincent had picked up the notebook I had laying on the table.

"Didn't anyone ever tell you it's rude to go through people's things?" I sighed.

"Probably," he admitted, not ashamed at all. "This is pretty awesome, though."

"Uh huh." I shook my head. It was an older sketchbook I had dug out. I was trying to find a specific drawing last night for Callie but it was still missing. Sighing, I picked up a more recent one. "At least look at one with actual good drawings." I traded them out before he could protest.

"For someone who said they weren't doing art things, you sure seem to have a lot of these out and about," he said as I put in the movie.

"I'm not working on making anything big or fancy. No paintings or portraits. Just some doodles here and there. Giving it up completely would be like giving up breathing." I started the movie. "But now we're onto the main event and ignoring my mindless doodles."

"Where's the fun in that?" He happily continued to look through the sketchbook.

"Pay attention and learn what a quality movie you're missing out on and get these songs stuck in your head for the next six months." I laughed as I sat down on the sofa.

Vincent sat next to me, still engrossed in the sketchbook.

I tugged it from his hands. "Movie time, bad drawings later."

"Fine," he relented and stretched out, putting his arms along the back of the sofa.

As the movie started I couldn't help but consider drawing now that the sketchbook was in my hands. I reached into the cushion and pulled out a pencil. One of the many I had dropped into it over the last two years of living up here.

Vincent glanced over at me. "So, I have to watch the movie but you can draw?" He seemed a bit too amused by this.

"I can repeat it word for word." I smirked right back. "The beginning is super cute."

"The prince pretending to be to a commoner?"

"And accidently bumping into the girl of his dreams." I agreed. "Not before a cute little musical number, of course."

"Of course." He watched the movie for a few moments. "Think anything like that could ever be close to real?"

"Sure," I replied honestly. "Why not? Some people grow to love one another, some get lucky enough to have those sparks fly from the beginning. Don't you think it's possible?"

"Yeah, I do." He nodded as he watched the movie.

Smiling, I went back to sketching. Vincent was easy enough to sketch sitting there. Thankfully, doing a profile only required drawing one eye.

"Are you going to watch any of this?" Vincent asked curiously after a few minutes.

"Shortly. Almost done." I looked up at him. "Now please go back to watching. You're ruining it."

Vincent raised an eyebrow but obliged. After several minutes, maybe more, I finished drawing, closed the book, and tossed it on the floor.

"I don't even get to see it?" He stared in shock at the sketchbook on the floor.

"After the movie." I smirked.

"That's not very fair." He crossed his arms.

"But this is one of the best songs of the movie!" I insisted, jumping right into the song. "...for a plain yellow pumpkin to become a golden carriage."

"So, you're using the song as an excuse?"

"And four white mice are easily turned into horses." I continued ignoring him.

"You're impossible." He grumbled at me.

"Impossible things are happening every day!" I smirked, continuing on with the song.

"You're definitely something." He laughed at my continued attempts at singing.

"What's that supposed to mean?" I asked.

"Oh, not a line of song for that one is there?" A sly smile crossed his face.

"You've got me there." I turned back to the movie.

"Is he not going to realise it's the girl he met in the marketplace like six scenes ago?" Vincent sighed.

"In the movie it was several days ago, if not longer. Just watch. He realises she's familiar but can't figure it out just yet." I pulled my knees up into my chest. "I love the ball scene."

"Fancy balls like this are exactly how the prince's first reactions were. Stuffy, dull, and not worth the time." Vincent clicked his tongue.

"You've been to many?" I couldn't help but stare wide-eyed at him.

"Basically everyone who has lived near the palace has. It's still a thing. Fancy gatherings, old style balls, several with old style dances too."

"You can ballroom dance?" I was more excited than I should have been.

"Yes?" He seemed surprised by my excitement.

"It just always looked fun." I shrugged, bringing my excitement down a notch.

"They don't teach that around here?"

"Sure, in grade school, but nothing more than a few quick how to's and then back to normal gym. I'm sure there're outside classes, but really it's not worth the money at the moment."

"If you'd like I could show you," Vincent offered.

"Nah, it's fine. You've already done enough anyway."

"Friends can help each other out, can't they?" He winked. "Come on, it'll be fun."

"You're missing the movie." I laughed.

"You've missed half of it!" he countered.

"But I've seen it before, so it's fine," I tried to counter back.

"And I know how it ends, so it's fine." Vincent smirked.

"That's not very fair," I grumbled.

"Tell you what, I'll finish watching it if you dance with me. At least once. It'll be fun." Vincent put his arm around my shoulder.

I felt all the heat rush to my face. What was this? What was I supposed to do about this? Oh a reply. "Sure." Nailed it. Was it even audible? Whatever.

He just chuckled. Was that a good thing? Ugh. Did it even matter? Was I falling for this guy? My brain felt like it was melting trying to put coherent thoughts together into manageable sentences.

Of course, the movie was nearly over. All that there was to watch was a montage of people failing at admitting the shoe was not theirs and the moment the prince realized he had met Cinderella at the marketplace in the beginning of the film.

"Okay, the ending is cute," Vincent admitted as we watched all the pieces fall into place. "They got to bring up that cheesy line again, but in a satisfying way."

"See? It is a good movie." I smirked and got up. "Though I have to throw a load of a laundry in or nothing is getting done today."

"Does that mean I can finally see the drawing?" Vincent asked as he picked up the sketchbook.

"I had thought you would forget about that." I sighed. "Go ahead." I dragged my laundry basket over to the closet by the door. I had a small stackable washer dryer unit, but it got the job done. Shoving as many shirts as I possibly could in there, I got it started up and closed the door, not that it did much to muffle the sound of the machine. It was clanky and loud, but I was already used to tuning it out.

I glanced at Vincent who seemed really into the drawing and shrugged. "If you'd like to continue the movie marathon you can pick the next one." I walked over and grabbed the movie box.

"Sure." He looked up from the drawing. "This is pretty good. A quick sketch and you got all this detail in?"

I shrugged, not sure how to respond. "Practice I guess?" I handed him the box filled with movies.

He started looking through them when he seemed to realize something. "Oh, I was going to show you some ballroom dancing."

"But.... movies?" I gave the box a small shake.

"Is this your way of saying you're afraid to dance?" He smirked.

Well, close... I shrugged. "I'm not afraid, I'm just not good at it, and it's silly to worry about when it's not going to be put to use."

"And what if you get into a great school and it comes up? The fancy schools by our lovely monarchs tend to have these sorts of dances." Vincent seemed to have too much of this conversation planned out.

"A problem for another day then. First issue is even getting into such a fancy school. Then there's too many extra problems to worry about. So forget it."

"Like what?" Vincent asked, hardly looking discouraged. "What else could be a problem? Say, for argument's sake, you get into said fancy school."

Easy. "Dress, and date. Dresses are stupid expensive."

"You have illusion magic." He shook his head.

"Yes, and while that can be used to my advantage here, a place where magic is more common it wouldn't fly. Too many could see right through that illusion."

"Not if you're better than them," Vincent argued.

"That's unlikely any time in the near future. Try as I might, there's still a lot of practice to go." I hoped this would help my argument.

"Guess you'll just have to practice both, then." Vincent smirked, still undeterred.

"Why are you so interested in this? I can get the wanting to help with magic stuff, but dancing? You didn't even sound interested in it at first." I crossed my arms.

Vincent set the box of movies aside and stood up. He mimicked my pose. "Maybe because I thought it would be fun to dance with you."

"Why would it be fun to dance with someone who can't dance?" I didn't get it.

He clearly saw I didn't understand and smirked even more. Was that even possible? "Because you make things fun."

I wasn't sure how to respond which only seemed to make him smile. What was he saying there?

"Come on, it'll be fun." He grabbed my hand and pulled me to the area between my sofa and the door. There really wasn't space for ballroom dancing room here, but that didn't seem to bother him.

He wasted no time getting into the basic steps, most of which I thankfully remembered. It didn't feel like much time had passed, but the next thing I knew it was already dark and my stomach had some unpleasant comments to make about a belated dinner time.

We had just stopped to get something to drink. "I can't believe it got so late." The clock happily said it was after seven. It was almost mocking me since I hadn't even completed a load of laundry. I moved over to the closet to put things into the dryer and start another load.

"Time flies when you're having fun." I could hear the smirk in his voice.

I rolled my eyes but finished getting my laundry started. "So they say. This couldn't be your idea of weekend fun."

"Close enough. It's not like there's a lot of options at the end of winter. Though at least it's supposed to be getting warmer this week." Vincent leaned against the kitchen counter. "Do you like living here?"

I laughed. "Have I given an inclination that I do?"

"Not really, but figured it wouldn't hurt to ask," Vincent mused.

I went and picked my cup back up, not sure what else to say. We stood there in silence for a moment as I sipped on my water.

"So, do you have things to get done tonight?" I asked.

"Sort of. I have to put a few plans together, but I'll probably just do that in the morning." He glanced over at me. "I suppose I should make sure I'm not imposing by hanging out all day."

"Not at all. Wish there was something more entertaining than movies and old games here." I shrugged. It wasn't bad having company once in a while.

We stood there silent again for a moment.

"Well, do you want some pizza and maybe watch another movie? Or...?" I let the last part trail off, not sure what else to suggest.

"That sounds good to me," Vincent happily agreed. "I suppose the offer still stands for me to choose a movie?"

"Sure," I agreed as he walked back to the sofa and I set the oven.

The movie went too fast and sadly I had to call it a night. Work was going to start far too early. Didn't it always, though?

Monday started with a headache. I was explaining just how much of one when Vincent joined Callie and me for lunch.

"I really don't know why my stepmom wants to do dinner tonight." I groaned.

"Hopefully not to set you up on a date again," Callie mused.

"What's going on?" Vincent let his confusion show.

"Stepmom wants everyone home for dinner. She didn't give a why, but it's usually something stupid when she tries to wrangle me back home," I explained.

"Wasn't last time to try and set you up with Ethan?" Callie tried to recall.

"I think that was the time before... Anyway, I'm pretty sure I made it clear I am not to be set up. Though when have they actually listened..." I sighed loudly.

"Can't recall a time." Callie shrugged, gathering up her things. "Keep me updated."

"As always." I waved her off.

"This sort of thing happens often?" Vincent continued to try and figure out what was going on.

"Every couple of months. It usually involves some sort of event I need to go to so stepmother looks like she has a wonderfully loving family or something about connection building, and on occasion trying to set up dates for me with someone that's family approved. I'll suffer through events, but I'm done with this matchmaking crap."

"I'm glad you're working on getting away. They don't seem to have any respect for you." Vincent seemed angry on my behalf.

"They don't and they never will. I just hope I'm in a good spot to apply elsewhere for fall semester but really, it'll be tough with all the random expenses that keep piling up."

"Well, I was going to show you this later, but I think you'd like to see it more now." Vincent replied as he scrolled through his phone. "Here it is." He passed over his phone.

He was right, I had to smile at the article but it wasn't the first time this had been proposed. Free school to students in good standing. Students with less than a 3.0 would need to pay some, but it was way better than now. Applying to get into schools was much the same, but still. A chance to go anywhere.

"Hopefully they actually pass it this time around. Even if they did, it wouldn't take effect until next year." The truth sucked.

"I think there's a good chance. It's a much better bill, and has a lot of important people supporting it." Vincent's excitement didn't diminish.

"Guess we'll see then. Doesn't fix much of the current problems though." I wish I could be more optimistic but it was just too hard.

"I bet there's a lot of good things in your future." Vincent nudged me.

"Oh? What makes you say that? I'm pretty sure the immediate future is going to involve another fight with my stepmom and probably a very lousy argument with Di. I doubt I'll get home without a headache."

"Well, miss grumpy barista, there's still plenty of time this year for things to go right. I'm going to keep betting that they will. Even if tonight isn't one of them."

At least he knew tonight wasn't going to be a good one. "All right, guess we'll see. If I'm right I'll keep my crabby title, and if I'm wrong I get to be pleasantly surprised. There's really no downside to this."

"There is no downside because I know things will go well." Vincent smirked.

"Uh huh. You can't tell the future," I pointed out.

"Don't need to to know this one."

I raised an eyebrow at him and just shook my head. "As much as I'd love to continue this argument, I must be off." I grabbed my bag and headed out.

"It's not an argument. Just a series of facts," Vincent called after me.

I just laughed for a moment before turning to wave back at him. "Well, as fun as it is to prove people wrong, I would like for you to be right."

"See? Just need to believe a little and it'll all come together." Vincent was smiling far too much. Could he really know something?

"Uh huh. See you tomorrow. If I survive this family dinner that is." I waved once more as I headed off.

While I knew dinner would go badly, I wasn't expecting it to start the second I was in the doorway.

Diamond didn't even let me get my shoes off before she began screaming at me for going out somewhere with Vincent. I hadn't noticed her friend Malina was there, but photo evidence was more than enough to not be able to deny it. Why should I?

"So what?" I was surprised at how loud my voice was in the entryway of the house. I hadn't meant to yell, well not that loudly anyway. "He helped me with my car, so I treated him to breakfast." I fudged the facts a bit there. It made for a better story. Not that I should need one but with psycho sister and a stepmom that supports these moments I was backed into a corner.

"He is mine. You don't even deserve the men we've tried to set you up with. You are plain, boring, and unable to do anything other than mop a floor. You'll never amount to anything." Diamond's glare was icy, but it did nothing to cool my rage.

Being plain wasn't a bad thing. I didn't think I was that boring. Oh no! I could handle chores! I had no reason to be ashamed. "If I won't amount to anything, then why are you worried?" I called her out on her fears. "If I'm so boring, then why are you upset? No one would spend time with me."

"That's enough," Stepmom called loudly from further inside the house. She quickly made her way to the scene of our argument. Her ink dark hair was pulled back into a tight bun which only made her sharp features look more stern than motherly. Rose stayed several steps behind her, watching the drama with glee. Diamond smirked at me while stepmom continued to criticize me. "You clearly have too much free time if you're stealing your sister's boyfriend. Your off time can be better spent here instead."

Yeah, he wasn't her boyfriend but whatever. "I am not stealing anyone." My tone was flat, I could only imagine the 'this is stupid' face I was making at them. "Not to mention he's going to be leaving this week anyway. I won't be seeing him again. Your concern is ill spent. I will see you at work tomorrow." I turned around and headed out the door.

"I am not done speaking with you!" I could hear my step-mother right behind me. I had no doubt Diamond was also on my heels.

"I'm done listening!" I called back, spinning on my heel to face them and walk backwards. "You're yelling at me for something that isn't a thing. I'm going to finish homework and get to bed. As usual."

"You will do as I say and come back here." Stepmother came to a stop, causing Diamond to nearly run into her.

I ignored her; instead I turned around to walk normally.

"You better listen to Mother." Diamond surprised me with a shove. I hadn't even heard her run up.

I stopped and turned around to face her. "I will listen about work things, but this isn't work. This is nonsense. I'm not stealing anyone, I'm going home."

Rose shook her head. She was still lingering just inside the door. "Sounds like lies to me..." Her singsong voice floated toward me, but I ignored it and continued on back to my car.

"If you take one more step you'll regret it." Stepmother's eyes turned dark, almost black.

I could hear the magic in her voice, wrapping around the words as she said them. I wasn't sure what she could do anymore. I knew her magic was weaker than mine, but illusions didn't solve family drama. My heart raced. What was she plotting?

Her influence in the town could get her out of most trouble, and hadn't helped me a bit after the other misadventures... This could go horribly. I felt panic bubbling up inside me. I needed to leave. Now.

"Just let me go home." I couldn't mask the terror in my voice. I tried taking several steps back away from them before I felt something tangle around my legs, causing me to slip as if I was on ice. I tried to brace myself and landed on my arm wrong. The crunch was loud enough to hear.

Tears filled my eyes as I cried out. The smile on both my stepmother's face and Diamond's was too much to look at. Their laughs rang with victory.

CHAPTER 7

Broken bones were a setback I couldn't afford, and yet now had to. The lovely step monsters weren't going to pay for the damage, and easily assured me on the ride to the hospital it was all my fault. If only I had listened, none of this would have ever happened. If I listened better, maybe I wouldn't be so broken. I needed time to heal and think about my actions. There really wasn't a choice in the matter. The ever lovely step monster declared it so. I needed time to think about what I had done to myself. So, nothing but school and rest for me.

Stepmother refused to let me work, out of the goodness of her heart. My eyes couldn't roll back any harder at that comment. The only good thing was the cast I had to wear had magic woven into the fibers. Instead of three months being out of commission, it was only three weeks. Just enough time to complete the school year a mess. It would take too long to replenish my savings now to go anywhere in the fall.

My heart ached for my father. I missed him and all he had done to try and keep my life together. He was gone though, so with the morning sun, I tried to force thoughts of the past away from my mind. I couldn't let it get to me now. I just couldn't...

I had told Callie everything last night, but wasn't sure what to say to Vincent. He'd notice quickly I wasn't at work. Still, I waited until after nine to send him a message.

"Won't be working today." Well, lame as it was that was a good start.

"That doesn't sound like you." Came the response.

He wasn't wrong. I didn't know what to say back. After a few moments he added another message.

"What happened?"

Might as well just get into the details. Or the details I could give. *"Slipped on ice last night. Broken wrist. The wonderful stepmother won't let me work until it's healed."*

There was a long pause before he finally replied. *"Did you actually slip or did something else happen?"*

Now that was the question of a lifetime. *"No one pushed me if that's what you're asking. Magic may or may not have been involved. I really don't know. Either way, no evidence of foul play."*

Another long pause before he replied, *"Are you going to head to school early then?"*

"Yeah. Step monster hid my keys until I'm healed too so I'm waiting on Callie." I hated that move of hers, but really it only made school and grocery shopping annoying. I didn't go many places.

"You're an adult. She can't take your keys." True, and yet, where were they? Oh yeah, in her hands.

"It's not worth the fight, Vincent. There's nothing to do in town anyway. I'm more upset that I can't work. I can't even try to make up for what this cost me."

It was a clear powerplay by the step monster. How to keep me under her control? Keep me broke and stuck here.

"Is there anything I can do to help?" I stared at his message. Was there anything?

"I don't know. I'm just tired and crabby today. I don't think anything other than a good night's sleep will help that one."

"Well, I've got a few ideas," he replied.

"Don't worry about it. It's just a broken wrist. It'll be fine in a few weeks."

When he didn't reply, I had a feeling he wasn't going to listen.

Vincent didn't show up at his normal time at lunch. Instead, I saw him stop Callie when she was on her way to her second class. They talked for a few moments, turned away from me so I couldn't even guess at what they were talking about before Callie had to rush off.

"What was that about?" I asked Vincent as he sat down next to me.

"Nothing important." He smirked.

"Uh huh. Because hiding it makes it totally unimportant." I shook my head.

"Pretty much." He winked. "I've actually got to head off in a few minutes but I wanted to see how you were doing and say I hope you feel better."

"I'll be fine." I shrugged.

"I'm sure you will be. Still, I got you something." Vincent pulled out a box and handed it to me. "I'll see you later."

With that, he was gone. Weird. I looked at the small box in my hands. It wasn't particularly heavy but did have a little weight to it. Curiosity finally getting the better of me, I opened it. I had to laugh. Inside was a necklace and a ring. The necklace was a pretty purple pendant. The second I picked it up I knew what it was. It warmed quickly at my touch and reacted with the inactive magic within me. A magnistone. It was a specialty stone used to help amplify abilities. It wouldn't be allowed in for exams, but it was something fun to have. I'd be able to practice longer without being tired and use more magic in general.

The ring was a different story. I had seen several rela-stone rings. They were mostly used to ward away magics used on you in a negative way. It was hard to say if one was real or not until you put it to use. I had a feeling it was real, though. A little good luck against magics that might harm me was exactly what I needed. Only yesterday. Still, it couldn't hurt. I put them both on and headed up to the library.

By the time I met up with Callie again, I had figured out how to perfectly illusion them so you couldn't see them.

"Ready to head back?" She asked brightly.

"Not really, but sure. Only if you tell me what you were chatting with Vincent about." I gave her an innocent smile.

"Oh, that." Callie laughed. "He asked for my number."

"Why?" That was interesting.

"Can't say. You'll find out." She looked far too amused.

"But you love telling me all the good gossip!" I tried to plead.

"That I do. This time I'm willing to make an exception. Also, I promised so…." She shrugged but kept smiling.

"Ugh. Come on. What are besties for?"

Callie shook her head. "Many things. And for once I get to do something fun for you."

"What sort of fun?" I tried to ask as sweetly as possible.

Callie covered her mouth and shook her head.

"You're no fun." Grumbling, I gathered up my bag.

She laughed and let down her hands. "Come on."

Not having to work helped me to get my homework done early, which left me a lot of nothing to do. I still had use of my hand, but it was crazy hard to sketch with the restrictive cast so instead, I put on a movie.

My phone chimed and I was far too excited for something else to focus on.

"Are lessons still a thing?" Vincent asked.

I hadn't thought of it. *"Sure. My arm might be broken but not my magic. Might as well do something if you're up to it."*

"Perfect. I figured I should double check but I thought of that after I got here, so I'm here."

I had to laugh. At least he tried.

I went down to the door to let him in and noticed he had a very full looking backpack. He normally didn't bring anything.

"What did you bring?" I locked the door behind him.

Vincent gave me a smirk. "Stuff." He shrugged before frowning.

"What's wrong?" I was surprised by his quick change of expression.

"You're hiding your necklace?"

"I didn't want to deal with family questions when I got back." I let the illusion fall. "Even more so with Diamond calling you her boyfriend."

"Oh, hell no." Vincent shuddered at the thought.

"Right? Had a feeling you wouldn't like that idea." I lead the way upstairs.

"That's so..." I turned to see Vincent trying to shake off the disgusted feeling that had overcome him. "I can't believe she'd say that."

"I can." I opened the door to my flat. "She's something. Though it doesn't appear that willing it to happen is working for her."

"I could never date someone like her." Vincent followed me into the flat and shut the door behind us.

"Then like who? Not that it's a challenge to beat 'miss I only want you for your looks'." I sat on the sofa and waited for the answer.

Instead of responding he stood near the door looking absolutely confused.

"I didn't think this was a trick question." I chuckled and took a seat.

"Then you answer it." He smirked, the confusion quickly slipping away.

I tried to answer then shut my mouth. Did I even have a type? I hadn't given it any thought in years. "I suppose we'll ignore this question and go back to an earlier one."

"And what's that?" He asked coming to finally sit by me.

"What's in the bag?" It was clearly stuffed to the brim.

"Stuff." He continued to smirk.

Of course, it was stuff. I rolled my eyes. "What specific kind of stuff?"

"The odd assortment kind." Vincent tried to hold back a laugh.

I stared blankly at him… or tried to. "Of course. The odd unnamed assortment kind." I crossed my arms.

"Aw no fun, you look too serious." Vincent grumbled and started to open the bag. "Wait, close your eyes."

"Why?" I asked suspiciously.

"Obviously it's a surprise."

"The entire bag is a surprise at this point!" I grumbled, frustrated.

He gave me a pointed look until I finally covered my eyes.

"This is stupid." I grumbled at him.

"Probably, but keep them closed." I could hear the amusement in his voice.

The sounds of things being removed from the bag made me give a careful, curious look. Only to see a wall of black in front of me.

"That's cheating. If you were going to use magic to hide things, why did I need to close my eyes?" I grumbled in defeat.

"As a backup in case you looked." He snickered.

I groaned loudly. "Not fair!"

"I had a feeling surprises weren't your thing. Hopefully, you won't hate me for too many surprises."

What did that even mean? "What do yo–" and just like that, the magic dropped.

In front of me was a purple stuffed floppy-eared rabbit. Vincent was already getting up, carrying a handful of things.

"What are you up to?" I asked, picking up the super soft plushie.

"Making a surprise dinner. I'm sure you're not feeling up to much, so I thought it might help cheer you up."

"You've already done more than enough." I laughed, not really sure what else to say or even how to react to all of this. I glanced over at him as he tried to find the pans he was looking for in my cabinets.

"Nah, this is nothing." He shrugged. "A little positive to combat this terrible event."

"Thank you…" I replied and looked back at my new bunny. It was cute, and very soft. Snuggling it close, I decided to hit play on my movie and wait to see what dinner would be.

It didn't take long for Vincent to finish dinner. In less than fifteen minutes he sat down on the sofa next to me and handed me a bowl. I stared at the chilli a little surprised by the choice. A delicious idea, and even better that I hadn't needed to figure out something myself.

"It's a dish I made a lot when I was in school. So, up until last year." He laughed, stabbing his fork into the bowl. "Spaghetti covered in chili. Easy, warm, and very filling comfort food."

That did sound pretty good. "How did you go from just being in school to touring schools?" I asked, digging into the meal.

He shrugged. "It's complicated and a rather boring story on top of that."

"So, boring as in you don't want to explain or you don't think I want to listen?" I asked, taking another big bite of food. It was really good.

Vincent took a bite as he considered my question. "I don't feel like explaining it. The short of it is, my mom found this great opportunity and had me take it. I didn't really have a valid reason not to, and it hasn't been all bad but... ugh. I'm so done with traveling."

I could see the tired look in his eyes. "Then why come back in a few weeks? Couldn't you use that time to go home instead?"

Vincent smiled at me. "Yes, but that'll ruin all the fun."

"What fun?" That wasn't even close to an answer I was expecting.

"Your school does an end of the year dance," he stated.

"Yeah, one that most of the school does not attend." I laughed. It was terrible, done on a dime budget, and had a CD player for a DJ. I had no idea where they got half the CDs from either.

"Since I know you have had zero cares about current school events, I'll fill you in." Vincent laughed. "So, somehow the Prince got roped into agreeing to crown a king and queen of the ball, so it's turned into a big thing."

"Damn, poor guy. This might be the first worthwhile event this town has had in a while." I laughed.

"But what does this have to do with you coming back?"

"I thought a dance could be fun. Would you like to go with me?" He smiled.

Yes, yes I would, but I could already see all the trouble that would cause. I glanced down at my cast.

"I won't let them hurt you again," I heard Vincent say softly. Glancing over, I saw how serious he was.

"I'll be okay." I tried to smile, but I knew it faltered.

Vincent leaned over and gave me a half hug. "I'm sure you will. Just a little more good luck and things will be fine."

We continued to eat in silence for a few moments.

"I think it would be fun to go with you. I'm sure you get my hesitation though," I finally said.

"Of course. Your family is nuts. But, I think things will work out," Vincent stated confidently. "Finished with your dinner?"

Nodding, I handed him the empty bowl. "How can you be so sure?" I didn't feel nearly as positive.

"Now that one I will keep a secret for now," he replied as he took the dishes to the sink.

I sighed loudly. "For someone I talk to a lot, there sure seems to be some crazy secrets going on."

"It's all just one secret." He laughed, cleaning up the dishes.

Just one, that everything ties to. Uh huh. Perfect. I grumbled to myself before deciding to put on a new movie. Shortly after, Vincent joined me again.

"I'm guessing you're not really up for any lessons, are you?" He asked.

I shook my head. "Nah, I thought I was, but I am starting to feel really tired."

"I'll let you get some sleep then," Vincent said getting up.

Without thinking I grabbed his arm, not letting him get up all the way. I quickly let go, not sure what to say next. What was even going on with my brain? I blushed.

"Want to watch a movie then?" Vincent smiled, not bothered at all.

"Sure. I think that sounds perfect," I agreed.

The movie played without us saying anything. I didn't know when it happened, but I ended up falling asleep. I woke up with a slight start when Vincent got up again.

"Sorry." I yawned an apology.

"No worries. You're tired. The movie's over; you should go to bed." I was glad he didn't seem bothered at all.

"K… you're probably ri–" My yawn cut me off. He got the idea.

Vincent laughed, scooped me up, and carried me over to my bed. "Get some rest. I'll see you tomorrow."

"But, I've got to let you out," I protested.

"As much as I'd normally agree, your backdoor is a push-bar that automatically locks, so I think I'll be fine to walk myself around." He smirked.

"I've got to get up and turn things off." I glanced around my flat.

Vincent sighed and shook his head. He went and turned off the tv, grabbed my new rabbit and handed it to me. "I can get the lights on my way out. Get some rest."

"Okay," I replied, giving up and laying down. My eyes shut against my will. Everything from last night through today had caught up to me. I heard him head out and I was quickly asleep soon after that.

CHAPTER 8

Wednesday morning went by quickly. Just mentioning the dance prompted Callie to get me up to speed on everything. Of course, it was Friday just after all finals had ended. That week was going to be a mess. People would be trying to study and prep for probably the only big social event this town would see for the next several decades.

The theme was 'Hidden Love' and the event was supposed to be a masquerade. It made me want to laugh and gag all at the same time. At least there was no 'ring before spring' nonsense floating around this year. Or was there? I hadn't actually been paying attention, and with the more recent events, I really didn't care.

Callie was already listing out the various thrift and craft stores within a reasonable driving radius and which ones we'd have to hit for the best sales. Vincent joined us just as Callie was jotting down more locations. His expression as he looked over the miniature map Callie drew and the scattered lists of facts and sale dates said it all. He clearly should have waited to join us.

"So, um, looks like you're excited for the dance." He gave a cautious laugh.

"I may not be the best at potions, but when it comes to thrifting and sewing, I've got this. I had so many pins saved online, I just know I'll find something that'll work for this dance," Callie replied, hardly looking up from her laptop as she continued to scroll, write something down, and scroll again.

"What she means is, she has enough ideas and things saved that she could probably make eight dresses, and still find something for someone that just happens to be laying around." I smirked.

Callie was in the zone. Not only did fabric bend to her will, but she had a good eye for clothes. She'd see the world's ugliest outfit and instantly know exactly how to make it work in a way that would make the best Pinterest queen jealous. Callie had three new offers for different fashion schools for next year, on top of the two from last year that she had declined. It was no surprise the declined ones re-sent an offer. Callie didn't feel ready to leave last year. This year, it was only a matter of choosing.

"Callie you've got class in ten," I reminded her.

"Hm? Oh." She glanced at the clock on her laptop. "Guess I should pack up, then."

"So, you're both going to the dance then?" Vincent asked.

I guess I hadn't given him a straight yes or no. Callie jumped in before I could say anything. "Of course, and we'll have some killer dresses, even if I have to design both of them myself."

"You really will." I laughed. "That is not my area of expertise."

"I never noticed." She smirked, finished shoving everything into her bag, and slung it over her shoulder. "Laters."

"Wait, what's that supposed to mean?" I glared at her retreating form.

"Darling, I'll make you look fabulous." She laughed, not even bothering to stop.

"Ugh." Was I that badly dressed or just constantly plain?

"So, you've decided to go, then?" Vincent asked, pulling my attention his way.

"Yes. I've no idea why you think things will work out, but I'd rather have some fun than stay home. But I can't promise I can dance well."

Well, at least he had a clear answer now. I knew there was no turning back once I brought it up with Callie. I did really want to go, I just hoped things could actually work out knowing Di and her gaggle would be there. Thankfully, it was limited to students and staff, so the step monster wouldn't be lurking as well, but that didn't ease my concern by much.

"You'll see. It'll be fun," Vincent reassured me.

"I don't know if I can share in your confidence." I hated to admit it, but there was no denying it.

To my surprise, Vincent grabbed my hand and looked me in the eyes. "So, there are several things I can't explain just this moment, but I promise I will when I get back before the dance. I hope you can just trust me on this. Even just a little." The passion with which he said those words made me want to believe him.

Could I though? "I'll try." He hadn't been dishonest or anything. It couldn't hurt to believe him a little. Too many little family 'accidents' came to mind, making it hard to really believe.

Vincent gave my hands a reassuring squeeze. "You'll see. Anyway, I've got to get going. Think you'll be up to lessons tonight?"

"Yes. I will actually be up for lessons tonight." I smiled. At least that much I could agree to.

Lessons went about the same as before. As did Thursday's. There was an odd tension building and I wasn't sure who was contributing to it more. Unsaid words, odd promises, feelings... At least I knew I had some feelings for him. Complicated as the whole mess of a situation it was, I liked him. I really, really, liked him. I wasn't about to admit it though.

Neither of us were clearly into the lesson concept on Friday.

"Want to just watch a movie?" I finally suggested. "You're leaving in the morning, right?"

"Basically." He shrugged. "It's weird, I've kind of gotten used to the area and now it's off to somewhere else."

"You can't say you'll miss it, though." I gave a half-hearted laugh and went to put on a movie.

"Yeah, you're right on that. There's not much here." He gave a small agreeing laugh in return. "But there's some people here I will miss, so it does make leaving hard."

I wasn't sure how to reply to that. I thought for the second I had while I put in a movie. "Glad not all of us are completely terrible." Well, that was lame. I retook my seat next to him on the sofa.

He chuckled and gave me a tight hug. "No, you're not terrible at all."

I blushed. "Sure I am. Terrible at dancing, terrible at removing glamor illusions, terrible at… finding better replies to things."

Vincent released me from the hug. Shaking his head, he just smiled. "You're not terrible at dancing, you're getting better with illusion magic, but yes, some replies are terrible. Terribly adorable."

I had no counter. He knew I had no counter and laughed.

"I'm going to ignore you now." I crossed my arms and stared firmly at the tv screen.

Vincent laughed for a moment. "Aw, come on. There's nothing wrong with being adorable."

Yeah, maybe? It really made it harder to reply. I could feel my cheeks get hotter and I was certain there was no way he didn't notice me blushing. Magic was useless to hide it at this point.

"Come on, don't ignore me," Vincent pleaded hugging me tightly again.

The change in tone, the desperate plea, and him suddenly being so close made me laugh. "Fine." I turned to look at him.

"You are adorable, you know," he stated with such honesty that I was once more lost for words. I was winning so hard tonight on the replies.

I just shrugged.

"It's true." He smiled.

"You're really cute too." Oh shoot, that wasn't inner dialogue. Um? How does one abort a social situation while in a hug?

Oh yes, by hugging more. I buried my face into his chest. Yes. Excellent plan.

After a moment Vincent hugged me tighter. "For someone who is normally not shy at all, this is extra adorable."

"You're not helping," I said into his chest.

"I can't hear you." Vincent chuckled.

"Good," I said a bit louder.

"Come on, it's hard to talk to you this way."

"Good." I laughed. Talking did not seem to be my thing tonight. At all. Ever.

He moved back some, but I hugged him tighter.

"Well that plan didn't work." He sighed.

My arm hurt in this position so I did have to move back. "Stupid arm," I grumbled.

"Aww…" Vincent looked down at the cast. "I hope you feel better soon."

"Soon… It'll thankfully be off before the dance, but it's so annoying." I sighed.

"Like someone hiding from you while using a hug as a shield?" He smirked, making light of the situation.

"No, that's not very annoying." Was I ever going to get away from this blushing? Maybe tomato red cheeks were the new in thing.

"True, but it does make it harder to talk," Vincent pointed out.

"What's there to talk about?" Why did I ask that? What can of worms did my lack of brain to mouth filter open?

"Well we can talk about the movie neither of us are watching or maybe the fact there seems to be some attraction here." Vincent gave a coy smile.

"I think I liked the awkward hugging better." Why didn't I just talk about the movie? Brain, work with me!

"I don't think there was anything awkward about it." Vincent laughed.

"My cast made it fairly awkward." Well, that seemed to be a safe enough comment. Half a point for you, brain.

"Hmm… Okay I can see that." Vincent nodded. "What would make it less awkward? Maybe the position? Maybe a one sided hug? If it's just me hugging then your wrist can't be bothered, right?"

Well two points to Vincent for keeping his conversation on track. Minus one to my brain for fueling it.

"Um… maybe?" I shrugged.

To my surprise, he pulled me onto his lap and hugged me tightly. "There. No awkward arm problems. Better?"

Better? In many ways, yes. In many other ways, no. I really hoped I was reading this flirtatious behavior correctly. This crush was *not* going to get any better after this. He did mention something about attraction so I had to be reading into this right. Right?

"Sure," I finally replied as I stared at the tv, not taking any of this movie in.

"That doesn't sound confident. Do you want me to move?" He sounded sad.

"No, no this is fine." This cuddliness was more than fine. "It sucks you're leaving."

He gave me a squeeze. "It really does."

For a few moments, we sat in silence. I couldn't tell what he was thinking. I hardly knew what I thought. He was leaving tomorrow and it sucked. I had no idea how we had gotten so close.

I was going to miss him.

A lot.

"I'll come back," he said after a moment.

"I hope so." I leaned my head back against him.

"I promise." He leaned his head against mine. "You can expect several texts. Maybe a few calls."

"I don't mind that." I smiled.

"Good." He turned to look at me. "Hopefully, it won't annoy you."

"Why would you annoy me?" I turned to look at him.

He shrugged. "Never know. You might get tired of me."

"Haven't yet. Don't think I just suddenly will." I laughed. Why were his eyes so dreamy? I could stare at them for hours.

For a moment we did just that. I wished I knew how to read him better. I wished I knew exactly what he was thinking. What he was feeling. Could I like someone so much so fast?

Vincent leaned his face in close to mine. "I think you're amazing," he whispered.

"You're the amazing one," I whispered back.

He moved his face even closer, and I met him for a kiss. It was exactly what I wanted, but I was so unsure. It had been so long since I had been close to anyone. Vincent didn't seem to mind. He was more than happy to take the kissing slow at first. My uncertainty quickly melted away as I felt his arms wrap reassuringly around me, allowing the kiss to build into something more.

When we finally pulled away, I wasn't sure what to say.

"This might be the wrong order of events," Vincent finally said, "But will you go out with me?"

I couldn't help but laugh, more like giggle at his statement. "Yes, I will."

"Okay. Good. That would have been terribly awkward if it was a no." He blushed.

I laughed. "Yes, it really would have."

He laughed and hugged me tightly. "I need to work on my timing. Leaving tomorrow is going to suck."

"Yeah…" I sighed. It already did suck, and this just added to it.

"You'll still get to talk to me, though." Vincent offered a smile.

"That part is nice." I smiled back. "Though it still really sucks."

"I'll come back and make it up to you." He beamed. "It'll be fun."

"But how long will you be back for?" I hadn't bothered to ask yet, but this did change a few things.

"Long enough." He smirked.

"That's not an answer." I glared at him.

"It's part of that small secret I can't explain just yet." He shook his head.

"And why not? Magic got your tongue?" I continued to glare.

"Actually yes." He looked relieved.

"Oh…" I wasn't expecting that. "Magic promise not to say something?"

He nodded, unable to verbally admit even that much.

"Why is magic stupid at the wrong times?" I sighed. At least I understood how this problem worked. A simple woven spell could can only last so long, but until it wore off, or if the conditions were met sooner, the person had to keep their promise.

"To be fair, I wasn't expecting it to be an issue. I was completely expecting this to be one of the more boring trips. Sometimes it's nice being wrong."

"Well, you really weren't. This place IS boring, and there's nothing here." I tried to counter.

"There's you." He held me close. "And I won't let you disagree with that."

"And how can you stop me?" I tried to cross my arms. Which was much harder when being hugged.

"Well, it's not really polite to talk over you or drown your words with a kiss, but I will keep countering you until you can believe how amazing you are."

That was better than most romance movies. Would it be wrong to want to kiss him for that? How did one relationship?

"You're too stubborn," was the best reply I could come up with.

"Not nearly as stubborn as you." He smirked.

"I'll gladly accept my title as Queen of Stubbornness. You may accept my title at any time." I smirked back.

"As Your Majesty wishes." He laughed. Vincent's phone made a few chirpy chimes before he sighed. "I actually do need to take that really quick."

I moved so he could get up.

With another sigh he answered the phone. "Hi, Mom." Ah, well that might be an important one. "Yes, I know. I've got just about everything packed."

He paused while I assumed his mom talked and strolled around my flat. "Yep, and yes, but can I–" There was another long sigh. "I'm actually going to have to call you tomorrow–" Vincent nodded a few times. "Because I'm spending some time with–" He rolled his eyes. "Yes, exactly. The girl I mentioned. Yes, so I'll call–" With a final nod he finally closed it out. "I love you too. Goodnight, Mom."

"It's probably about time for you to go isn't it?" I stated. It was starting to get late.

Vincent nodded. "Probably, but maybe we can manage another movie? Though you're probably tired."

"You're the one who has to drive tomorrow. I've got nothing going on." I waved my casted arm. "Whatever is fine by me."

"Well, what do you want to do?" He asked, coming to sit back on the sofa.

"Be greedy and keep you here longer," I replied honestly. It was probably the least worst thing I had admitted all night.

"Another movie it is." He smiled.

"Your pick." I laughed. "My pick apparently wasn't entertaining enough."

"I think it was a worthwhile distraction." He smirked as he went and put on something different.

"No complaints." I blushed, glad his back was turned to me.

After he joined me on the sofa, we cuddled together and watched the movie. Some of it, anyway. I knew I was getting too tired, but didn't want to send him off so I could sleep. Instead we both fell asleep.

I was surprised to wake up at three in the morning to find we were both still on the sofa. The movie screen was still happily lighting up the room. Carefully I nudged Vincent awake.

"Wake up, sleepy head." I yawned. Yep, I sounded convincing.

"Hm?" He cracked an eye open at me. "Sorry did I fall asleep?" He yawned and finally opened both eyes.

"It's three." I nodded and replied with another yawn.

"Oh. Wow." He glanced at his phone to confirm the time. "That was unexpected."

"You should get back so you can leave on time tomorrow." My voice sounded way sadder than it needed to. I tried to smile to make up for it, but it faltered.

"I'll miss you too." He hugged me. "But yeah. It's way late, and I should pretend to be somewhat of an adult."

"It's three a.m. Who really adults at three a.m.?" I protested. I could feel a yawn creeping back up. I was too tired to fight this silly battle.

"No sane person." He kissed my forehead. "You need sleep. I promise I'll call."

"Okay…" I wasn't sure how I felt, but I knew this was coming.

Tiredly, we walked to the door.

"I'm glad I could have such a great last night here with you." Vincent hugged me tightly as we lingered for another moment.

"Please drive safe." I buried my face in his chest.

"I will. Please be careful." He hugged me even tighter for a moment. "You can call or message me anytime."

"Okay." I mostly had responded to his messages. I guess I could initiate some. I looked up at him, not sure what else to say.

Instead of more words, we kissed. A slow kiss at first, but it quickly built to a powerful goodbye. Finally, he had to go.

Tomorrow was going to suck.

CHAPTER 9

Except Callie didn't give the day much time to suck. The second she called to arrange plans for thrifting, I filled her in on the details of last night. Few as they were, it was squee-worthy enough for her to be ready to go in half the time. With coffees in hand, we were quickly on the road.

"I think this is going to be an awesome dance," Callie mused as she pulled onto the highway.

"It'll be something for sure." I laughed. "I've no idea how this will go. Having a date is one level of nonsense I wasn't expecting, and it'll be an extra notch of crazy with the prince there. How was his seminar thing, anyway?"

"He's fun. I loved his presentation. I bet it'll go fine enough for any of us not pining over his attention." Callie seemed to be in the same mindset as me about all that royal nonsense.

"That reminds me, you never did show me it." With all that had gone on this week, I had completely forgotten to ask.

"It was great! He showed off some of his magic, too." Callie pulled out her phone and handed it over to me. "It's the last video I took."

I stared at her phone for a moment before remembering her unlock pattern. "Oh, that's cool. Did he show off anything interesting?" I finally found the video and clicked on it.

"Just watch." She laughed and turned down the music.

After watching for a few moments, I noticed something. "His voice sounds crazy familiar."

"Well, he has been around campus. It wouldn't be surprising if you ran into him and didn't know it," Callie mused.

"Very true," I agreed, but couldn't shake the feeling it was more than that as the video continued on. "I wish you got closer, the sound quality sucks."

"Right? And I got there early. Geeze. I can't believe how crazy it was." Callie shook her head. "Oh well. We've got about a half hour before we get there, so let's get this karaoke party started!" She flipped the music back on loud.

Laughing, I turned off the video with the intent to watch it another time and joined in. Nothing made a road trip better than an overly dramatic duet, filled with terrible car dancing, and singing in octaves no one should attempt. In no time at all, we arrived at the first location.

And on the day went.

Callie was the dressmaking mastermind and so many times I just stared at something she'd pick up and wonder how she was ever going to make it work. Of course after the first two locations you'd think we'd be good. That's not how things worked with Callie. She wanted backup items and ideas in case something ripped or ended up not looking as she had planned. Five thrift stores and two craft stores later we finally headed back home.

The next few weeks became a mess of trying to help Callie with making dresses, holding still while she pinned things, class work, self-lead magic practice, and talking with Vincent when we were both free. Trying to both be free was more of a late evening adventure, making random messages throughout the day the best way to communicate. Or complain about school and life.

Finally, I got the message I had been waiting for.

"So, pending on some nonsense at home, it looks like I'll be back Wednesday the 9th."

Inwardly, I was cheering. *"Awesome, the day of my illusion final. If I don't survive it, please know that Callie helped to make an awesome dress for the dance. Or made the entire thing with little of my help…"*

It didn't take long for him to reply. *"I'm sure you'll do fine. You've been keeping up with practicing and you've read over my notes at least a dozen times. You've got this."*

"Maybe read it like eight dozen, but still. It's going to be a tough final. I really don't think half the class is going to make it." That much was true. I really

wouldn't be surprised if a third flat out failed and half got D's which wasn't a passing grade by far. Most of the schools I had been looking at wouldn't even accept the transfer credit unless it was a B or higher. Doing fine wasn't going to cut it.

"You were already more than ready for this final before I left. I have no doubt that you'll pass it at worst, and ace it at best. There's not a single technique you're struggling with."

I couldn't really argue it. There wasn't anything I was struggling with, but I wasn't confident enough to say I was good enough to ace this class. Still, I had been working really hard and hoped it would show.

Instead I chose to go back to the original comment. *"So Wednesday? :)"*

"Yes, if all goes well here, then Wednesday."

"The 'if all goes well' part isn't very reassuring." Yeah, that's not happening then.

"At the worst it'll be early Thursday. That shouldn't be the case, though," he replied.

Worst case would probably make the most sense. It was finals week, the week of the ball, and I'd finally getting to see my new boyfriend again. Thursday was totally going to be it.

"So, *what would keep you?*" I asked curiously.

"A *complex set of preparations that make sense only to my mother. If a mother can make a bigger deal out of a dance than necessary, she will.*" Now, that I could believe. I had already seen Henrietta the step monster going mad while finding Diamond the perfect dress, setting up appointments with the best hairdresser she could find, getting a makeup specialist, and making sure all the little odds and ends of tanning, nails, and whatnot were all in line. I was more than relieved they paid me no mind. I doubt they even knew I was attending. How could they when no one had bothered to ask?

"*It's just a dance, it'll be fine,*" I finally replied.

"*If it was just a dance then who'd make a big deal about it? Clearly, this is going to be one of the biggest events of a lifetime. LOL.*"

That was exactly what the majority of the school and town population were thinking. At least it should be fun with everyone actually putting some effort into it.

With finals to prep for and take, I didn't worry much about the final details of the dance until after everything school-wise was said and done. I had helped Callie all I could with the dresses. I was reasonably confident that I could do my nails, hair, and makeup well enough – and if need be, I would resort to my magic. Illusion magic was the perfect backup plan. Not that many eyes would be on me, anyway.

Thankfully, they would be all on our guest star, the prince, and anyone who might dance with him. I wasn't sure how someone could handle that much spotlight. Lucky for me, that wasn't my problem to know.

Once finals were over on Wednesday I felt like I could finally breathe again – and my cast was finally off! It felt so good to finally have full range of movement back. I decided to shake off the physical funk my arm was in and work on some sketching. It would probably still be several days before things felt normal again, but this was a great start. I was a third of the way through trying to figure out how to get a hand to look right when my phone went off.

"I'll totally be here today, but not until late."

Well, that was no surprise. *"What is late?"* That was the important question.

"*Maybe ten. So, I'll have to check in and stuff.*"
The lame truth about how hotels work.

I wanted to convince him to stop by after, but I
was sure he'd be tired. "*Since school's done, what
about breakfast?*" I wasn't back on the schedule until
next week, so I might as well enjoy this extra bit of
freedom while I could.

"*I'd love nothing more,*" was his response followed
by a quick second one. "*All right, back on the road
for me. I'll message you when I get in. Maybe we can
talk if you're up.*"

It was an excellent plan, except for the part where
I fell asleep. Instead, I woke up when the sun was
already shining brightly through my curtains and my
phone was ringing happily away.

"'Ello?" I mumbled, still trying to get the sand out
of my eyes.

"Morning sleepy head," Vincent's amused tone
came through.

"Why are you so happy in the mornings?" I grumbled, my brain not catching up with the fact I should
probably be happy.

"Because, I get to see you today. Isn't that enough
to be a morning person for a moment?"

"I'll let you know when I'm awake." I yawned. I was excited to spend time together again, but this grogginess was clinging to me something terrible.

"I'll take that as you're excited but need some time." He snickered.

"Yeah, maybe like…. No, make it an hour. That should be good enough." I nodded to myself.

"And I'm guessing picking you up might raise a bit of a problem." I could hear the caution in his voice.

"Probably. The easiest way would be just to wait in the parking lot. If you can just disguise your car to look like Callie's that'll be enough."

"Easy enough. Now, onto the next concern." Vincent hesitated.

"Probably the one where everyone in town knows me and we don't want another 'oh em gee, There goes Arnessa stealing Di's boyfriend again'."

"Ugh, that is still vile to hear." Vincent sounded repulsed by the thought.

"Isn't it? But yeah, I'll just use some illusion magic, be done with it. Any other worries?" I couldn't think of anything else.

"Nah, I think that covers it all." He sounded a lot happier now that things were decided.

"Perfect. I'll see you in an hour, then." With that, we ended the call and I dragged myself out of bed to get ready for the day.

Somehow, an hour went by too fast. The magical time warp called a shower was never the fifteen minutes I intended but somehow I was ready on time. I even had a chance to fix up my hair, which was more than I had done in weeks thanks to that lovely cast.

It was still a toss-up in my mind if I just misstepped on ice, or if magic was involved. From how happy my lovely stepmom was about the whole aftermath, I had a feeling she was involved. I wondered if there was any way to combat her on that level. Even if there was, did I want to be in a battle against her?

Nope.

She wasn't worth my time. There were too many things I wanted to accomplish. That I needed to accomplish in order to get where I wanted to go. She could delay me, but I was never going to let her stop me.

"Here." The lovely text chimed at me. With a happy spring in my step I headed downstairs.

"What are you so smiley for?" Diamond asked as I passed by the register.

Ummm, none of your business... but I bit my tongue. "Finishing things up with Callie. Gotta be ready for the dance tomorrow, right?" I shrugged and continued on.

"Why are you even going?" Diamond's face distorted with disgust as she contemplated me doing anything fun.

"Because I want to?" I thought this wasn't going to be a big deal. "We never have anything exciting in this town. A dress up night should be just the right thing to end the school year. I doubt you'll even notice me there."

Diamond nodded, her face shifting back to normal. "True. It's not like you have anything worthwhile to wear. I'll at least have more than a shot with the prince." Her smug expression said it all.

Oh, there was no way I'd let her see the dress. I wasn't big on fashion, but to me, it rivaled the ones I had seen in magazines. Callie had done an incredible job.

"Have fun with that." I waved her off and headed outside.

I couldn't help but laugh as I sat down in Vincent's car. I could not see the prince of all people being interested in anyone from this town, let alone the demon like creature my step-sister could be.

"What's so funny?" Vincent eyed me curiously.

"My sister is claiming she'll be dancing with the prince." I tried to shake off the laughter.

"Ugh, no." Vincent looked repulsed for a moment before leaning over and hugging me.

"Right?" I hugged him back. "How have you been?"

"Better now that I get to see you." He flashed his ever charming smile.

As cheesy as it was, I blushed. "So, um, what are you in the mood for?"

"Whatever you like. Your last suggestion tasted amazing."

While it was an easy cop out, I knew it was true, but sadly there wasn't a way to top it. I wasn't expecting us to ever become a thing. "Umm, I don't know what else will be amazing, but I've got an idea that is pretty good."

With that I navigated the way to another local fav, but this time made sure an illusion was in place before we got there. Auburn hair, hazel eyes, and some extra freckles were good enough.

"You're gotten really good at that," Vincent commented as we pulled into a parking spot.

I wasn't sure what to say. "I hope so. I have been practicing. Not to mention I had a really great tutor."

"I'm not sure if I'm that great a tutor. You just needed some extra practice and to have some fun with it. That classroom setting here is really lame for what should be a great class."

"Glad I'm not the only one who thinks so." I smiled at him. "Shall we eat then?"

The inside of this restaurant was small and it was always busy. We were lucky to get seated right away. As we sat down I noticed Vincent taking in the decor. They were trying so hard for a modern vibe but it felt forced. Every couple of years the family who owned it switched things up. The ones that stuck out in my mind were a country homestead a-la little house on the prairie, under the sea with an old divers suit and far too many starfish, and farmers market with so many plastic fruits and vegetables hanging all over everything you hardly saw wall space.

"This place is… different." He continued to glance around.

"Yes, yes it is. The menu will make up for it." I nudged his closer to him.

"Sure, why not." Vincent laughed and opened it up. "Sometime I'll have to return the favor. There's some great unique restaurants around Rosewood."

"I don't know how I'll ever make it up there." I sighed. Sure, it was the city right by the college of my hopes and dreams, but still. I didn't want to get my hopes up.

"We'll make it work out." Vincent flashed a confident smile.

"I've no idea how." Was this guy ever unsure?

"Maybe some magic, maybe some luck." Vincent shrugged, still smiling with the same confidence. "Maybe, just maybe, I've got a plan."

"What sort of plan?" What did he mean by that?

"You'll have to wait and see." His smile turned into a playful smirk. "I think it'll work out nicely, though."

"If you tell me I can confirm that thought for you." I smiled back. This could work, right?

"No need." He grinned. "Callie likes the idea, and if she's confident it'll work out, then I have no reason to believe it won't."

"Oh no fair. How is she in on something like this?" I remembered her saying she gave him her number. Annoyed, I pulled out my phone and sent her a message. *"What are you in on? What is Vincent planning?"*

"She won't tell you." He laughed.

"Callie is the worst secret keeper." It was my turn to smile confidently.

"Yes, she said as much, but as you know there are ways to keep secrets." Vincent gave a small laugh.

"Oh. You both suck." Freaking magic promises.

"I'll never tell!" Callie finally sent back. *"Besides, you'll find out soon enough."*

"I hate waiting on weird surprises," I grumbled at her.

"You don't have to wait long. Promise." Vincent laughed and went back to looking at the menu.

Sighing, I glanced at the menu and set it back down. I always got one of two things here. "Can I get a hint?"

Vincent glanced over the menu at me. "Sure. Let me think."

Before he could give one, the waitress came by and took our orders. I waited as patiently as I could for a hint. The seconds were taking too long to creep by.

"Okay, I've got it." He smirked at me.

"Well…?" I motioned for him to get on with it already.

"I like to be a royal pain with my hints, and make them hard to guess." He chuckled to himself. "My noble idea will make far more sense after tomorrow night."

"That's not a good hint." I frowned.

He shook his head and chuckled. "I think it works."

"I don't agree. At all. Whatsoever." I crossed my arms and glared at him.

"It'll be a fun surprise."

"Surprises aren't that fun." I continued to glare.

"I'll tell you what." He gave an evil grin. "What about a little deal?"

Interesting. "What sort of deal?"

"I've mentioned before I regularly use illusion magic. I know that's never bothered you, and you don't typically try to see beyond appearance illusions, or even try to break them." He smiled slyly. "But if you can find a way to break mine, I'll tell you."

Instantly, I felt out to the magic around him. It was layered and woven so tightly I knew it would be more than difficult to just dispel it. "That's not very fair," I grumbled.

"It's not impossible. Just extremely unlikely. Which is why it's perfect." He was a bit too proud of himself, that smirky jerk.

"This isn't perfect," I sighed.

"Well, if you manage it, not only will you get your answer, but you'll totally have proved me right about doing amazing for your final. And if not today, I'm confident you'll figure out how to do it soon enough. I'll make sure you master these gifts. Not to mention then I get to go through with my amazing plan." He shrugged and gave the sweetest smile he could manage.

"Fine, I guess there's not really another option," I relented.

"Perfect!" He beamed, a little too happy with himself. "So, what should we do for the rest of the day?"

"I have an idea. It's a pretty silly one though," I offered.

"Well, let's hear it."

"I was thinking it would be fun to keep some illusions up today. There's a lot of this silly little town you haven't seen, and some terrible touristy sites that aren't half bad. So, why not make a day of it?" It was cheesy, simple, and overall free. Having a low key day after exams sounded wonderful.

"That could be amusing. I really haven't taken in any of the sights in most places I've been, so why not?"

With that, our food arrived.

CHAPTER 10

y idea wasn't super exciting, and there was only enough to do to kill half the day. The river walk was cute but short. Still, walking together and holding hands made me giddy with joy and tremendously happy. Checking out the view of point tower that overlooked the river and almost the entire town was always fun. We spent more time there taking pictures than anything else.

What I was really excited for was the Lorelai Knapperick memorial house. The tour itself cost money, but walking the gardens was free and by far the best part of it all.

"The roses are my favorite," I explained to Vincent as we slowly walked through the different plants. "I love how she figured out how to use them to help harvest small magical energies. Their healing abilities are phenomenal."

"I didn't know you liked flowers so much."

"They're some of my favorite things to draw. I've come here so much and read the signs so many times… it became more than just fun facts to know. I enjoyed reading more on the different things here and what the plants go to when they are finally harvested." I shrugged as we continued to slowly meander our way along the trail. "I used to come here a lot when I was younger. It was probably a three or four-mile bike ride back then. Totally worth it."

"Can I ask you something?" Vincent asked. His tone took on a more serious note causing me to look up at him.

"Sure. What's up?"

"You don't have to answer of course. I was just wondering how long your step-mother has been like this…" He let the question drift off.

It wasn't a bad question, and not one that bothered me, but it did feel weird to explain. "She and my dad started dating when I was about seven or eight. She wasn't very friendly to me then, but she wasn't cruel. At least not in a noticeable way. It wasn't until my father got too sick when I was about fourteen that things really stood out about her personality. I don't know when exactly things completely changed. It wasn't slow, but it wasn't a sudden surprise either." I didn't know what else to say. I had never liked the woman, and she never liked me. Maybe because it was clear my father always put me first? Maybe not. Thinking back didn't present any hints or clues.

Vincent didn't seem to know what to say in response either so we walked in silence for a while. The garden was still easy to enjoy, and I happily pointed out my favorite flowers and took more photos with my phone along the way.

We finally reached the end of the garden with still plenty of time left in the day. "Any thoughts about what we can do now?" I glanced at the time. Only six.

Vincent paused at the exit with me while he thought. "Maybe dinner? I know I'm hungry."

I was hungry. All the walking around and sight-seeing made for a long day. "How about we stop at the store and get some things for dinner?"

"I'm fine with going somewhere too. I don't mind paying." He offered.

"As sweet and wonderful as that is, I'm not used to using this much magic all day." I shook my head. "Something quick and simple sounds wonderful."

"Chinese takeout?" He suggested. "That way it's quick and we don't have to make it."

"You win this one." I laughed. "Okay, let me find a menu…" I pulled up the restaurant on my phone.

It took almost no time to get food and get back home. It was a blessing that the shop closed at six, and thankfully there was no Diamond or anyone else lingering around after hours. Tomorrow would be a different story, but tomorrow's problems could wait another day.

"What are we even doing tomorrow?" I asked after everything else was done and we were considering putting on a movie.

"That's a great question. Ummm..." Vincent thought for a moment. "Tomorrow's an odd day. There're things I need to do before the dance since I somehow got roped into a long list of things." He gave a small laugh. "But you probably need to get ready anyway, so what about meeting up an hour before the dance?"

"That works for me." I shrugged. "What are you stuck doing?"

"More or less setting up things, making sure everything is done correctly as far as security goes," He shook his head. "Don't give me that look, just because you don't care about someone's title doesn't mean the prince isn't going to need all that nonsense."

I couldn't help but chuckle. "Fine, I guess he would be important enough to need some form of security around. Though he's probably good enough to magic his way through problems."

Vincent smirked. "Possibly. Though I'm sure the choice isn't always up to him. I wouldn't be surprised if he gets in enough trouble sneaking off with his magic when everyone important around him thinks he needs to be guarded."

Huh, did not think of that. "Maybe. Must be a weird life to live."

"Would you hate such a life?" he asked curiously.

"I don't know. It would be different I'm sure. I bet there's all sorts of stuffy boring stuff that's required, but it's not like anyone is exempt from those moments. I think I'd rather be bored attending a formal event than trying to figure out why deck scrubbing a floor with hot water and bleach is doing nothing to remove the filth." I shook the thought from my head, knowing next week would involve a lot of those moments. Diamond loved to cut corners. "I think the only big problem is the media, but I'm sure someone so important would have someone to help sort out that nonsense to some degree."

"What about all those fun meetings and having to keep up alliances? Maybe mopping is a bit better than that." He chuckled.

"Depends on who you're meeting with. I'm sure there's always going to be that person that would make you rather watch paint dry. Still, it doesn't sound like an awful existence." It was something interesting to think about. "What about you?"

"If I could occasionally slip past the guards, I think it wouldn't be too bad. I could handle it." He smirked.

"And what would a prince want to do so bad that he'd need to slip past the guards?"

"Well, really doing anything without having a gaggle of people following you would be the biggest thing. Maybe just the adventure of having a normal moment, pretending to be just like any other person for a while. Run off, accidentally fall in love, and be stuck in a hilarious situation where you're not sure how to confess anything."

"That could be hilarious, or heart crushing. That's a big secret to keep from someone. I guess it would depend on how that someone handles it." It would be such a cute tale, though!

"How would you handle it?" His smirk seemed less confident.

I shrugged. That was a tough thing to try and guess at. "No idea. I guess it would depend on if that was the only secret they kept. Hiding something like that for awhile would make sense. Too many people can change just over hearing a title." I shook my head. "It's a bit silly that it happens, but with how crazy everyone's been just for a glimpse at this prince, I can see why someone would hide it. You never know if you'll meet someone like Diamond or Callie. Diamond would do anything for the attention, but Callie would quickly get over the fame and glory moment and be wondering what material your shirt's made from and if it was infused with certain magical fibers or not."

Vincent laughed. "Well, I'm glad that's a normal Callie thing. I wasn't sure what to say to that question. Partly from surprise, partly because it's just a shirt."

"Isn't she great?" I loved how curious she was about the things she saw. "She probably knew more that than you did about it just from a glance."

"Would you get over the shock of fame just as quickly?" Vincent continued the topic.

"Probably?" I shrugged. How would I know? "It's anyone's guess, really. Important people are still just, you know, people. I can't imagine getting caught up for long in all that 'oh em ge! You're so famous' nonsense."

"I can completely see that," Vincent agreed. "So, what movie is on the agenda tonight?"

"I was thinking rematch on Smash Karts." I smirked.

"Oh, is that so?" He grinned. "Well, I won't be losing so easily this time."

"Your fancy magic doesn't make up for how much better I am than you," I teased.

"Bring it."

The night went by too quickly. At some point we had finally decided to switch over to a movie and cuddled on the sofa. Half asleep, I noticed Vincent was out cold. As much as I wanted him to stay, I nudged him awake.

"You should go to bed." I yawned.

He wrapped his arms tightly around me. "This will do."

As heartbreakingly cute as I found it, I had to disagree. "This sofa is not good to sleep on. You should get to a real bed, silly."

"But you're here, so this will do," he protested softly, almost back asleep.

"We'll see each other tomorrow. Come on." Reasoning didn't seem to be working.

"Nah…"

"I could finally just thwart your disguise instead." I snickered.

Yawning, he finally glanced over at me. "That's not fair, and no you can't."

"I could. You're too tired." I kissed his forehead.

"Nuh huh." He tried to say but it came out as more of a yawn.

"Challenge accepted." I shook my head. I could feel him try to resist, but he wasn't awake enough yet for that to fully work. In a few short moments the illusion was gone and I snuggled close to him once more. "See?"

For a moment he was surprised and much more awake. Then something dawned on him. "And you hardly gave me a look?"

"It was hardly fair." I yawned, actually looking at him now. His hair was a much darker brown now, almost chestnut, and his eyes more of a deep ocean blue. It didn't seem like a lot had even changed. "You're still just as cute." I buried my head in his chest.

He chuckled for a moment. "And nothing changes."

"You're still Vincent, right?" I mumbled into his chest.

"I seem to be," he mused.

"Then what would change?"

He was quiet for a moment. "Nothing, I suppose."

"There ya go." I yawned again and looked up at him. "But I think we both need sleep."

"Fine." He sighed as we moved to get up.

"Why don't you go by your normal appearance?" I asked as we reached the door. I couldn't find any reason against it, but magic was always an odd thing that some people just preferred to use.

"Because I don't always like to," he replied simply. "I think you'll understand more tomorrow."

What did that mean? "Why tomorrow?"

He leaned in and we kissed for a moment. "You'll see. Until then." He smiled and left.

Why were boys so strange sometimes? Shaking my head, I went to bed.

CHAPTER 11

On Friday, I slept in. It was after nine when Callie finally messaged me wanting to know when she could drop off the dress. Settling on soonish, I got up, tossed my hair up, and put on something presentable enough to sneak downstairs. Thankfully, it was just Steph manning the floor.

"I heard you're actually going to the dance," she called to me as I walked around to the customer side of the room.

"Thought it might be fun." I could only assume Di had been complaining about it. "So, Callie and I, well mostly Callie, put together some dresses."

"Ooo." Steph smirked as she started to make a drink. "Guess who is rather upset about that?"

"Really?" I raised an eyebrow and went to talk to her by the pickup counter. "Why the heck would Diamond care if I'm going or not?" I wasn't surprised she was complaining, but actually upset? There was almost zero chance we'd run into each other.

"Believe it or not, she thinks you're going to sabotage her."

"How? By wearing a custom altered thrift store find?" I rolled my eyes. "Please. Can't I just enjoy myself?"

"Nope. All joy belongs to that gem. If you're enjoying something, she must be doing something wrong." Steph laughed, handing me a drink.

"Whatever." I accepted the drink. "What's this?"

"Just a vanilla latte with some stress relief magic."

"Why relaxing?" I gave the drink a tentative sip.

"Because you'll need it if Diamond decides to be a bitch today, and you know she will." Steph gave me a knowing nod before stepping over to help a customer that had just walked in.

Shrugging, I slowly drank the latte as I watched for Callie.

When she pulled up, I met her at the door.

"Ready for tonight?" She was bubbling over with excitement.

"Sure. It'll be fun." I shrugged, feeling a little less excited knowing Di might try and start something.

"You're the worst morning person." She sighed, taking the excitement down a notch and handed over the dress.

She had it hanging up and in a clear bag. The blues and greens of the high-low dress caught my eye.

"I do really love this dress. You did amazing."

Callie beamed happily. "I know. It's fantastic. Send me pics when you finally get it on!"

"Will do. Thanks again." I gave her a quick hug and we parted ways.

When I turned to head back I noticed Diamond was back on the register and trying hard not to glare at me. Well, Steph was right. I was hoping more along the lines of 'you shouldn't bother going' texts, but I guess I'd deal with the cards I was dealt.

I did my best to ignore her as I walked by.

"That's the trash you're wearing tonight?" She scoffed at me.

I turned to see her raised eyebrow and crossed arms. "Yep, it's cute, but couldn't afford to go all out fancy. At least it'll be fun."

"You think that is cute?" Her face wrinkled with disgust. "No wonder you can't land a guy."

No wonder you can't keep a guy, but I kept the thought to myself. Instead, I shrugged and continued on my way.

Upstairs, I set the dress out on the bed and started to look for the deep blue flats I had that would look perfect with it. After a few minutes of shuffling things around, I found them and went to hop in the shower. Halfway through shampooing my hair, I felt a weird tingle of magic. I didn't know what was going on, but knew it had to be Henrietta. What could the step monster be up to? Probably something for Diamond since she'd be needing to get her hair and whatnot done soon.

As soon as I stepped out of the shower a sense of dread gripped me. The only thing keeping me upright was the magic from the latte earlier. What could have happened?

I opened the door from my bathroom and my jaw dropped in a silent scream. The dress was everywhere. Shredded to bits. Cut, torn, and ripped to pieces. Even my flats were cut apart. Why would they do this?!

I sunk to the floor, trying to hold the towel tightly around me. There was no way I could go now. I finally had a chance to do something exciting, different, fun and…

It was all torn apart.

On the counter, I could hear my phone buzz. Slowly, I forced myself up to look at it.

"Can't wait for tonight." Vincent had messaged me.

Well… you're going to have to. The feeling of defeat was crushing. I didn't even know what to tell him.

With shaking hands, I called Callie instead.

"What's up?" I heard her voice say.

"They ruined it all…" I wasn't sure if she even heard me at first.

"Give me an hour." She clicked the phone off before I could even reply.

I didn't know how long I stood there before I finally texted Vincent.

"*I don't know how tonight's going to work,*" I typed, not sure if I should send it at first. Maybe Callie could save the day here. I sent it and added, "*They ruined my dress, but Callie seems to have a plan.*"

After a few minutes, he replied. "*I'm so sorry. Are you okay?*"

"*Me? Yeah, nothing happened to me. Just the dress, and my shoes. Everything is destroyed. Callie just said to give her an hour. I don't know what she's planning. Hopefully, things can still work out.*" I wasn't feeling too optimistic. Maybe I should have asked for a luck boost.

"*They will. Dress or not, I'd still love for you to be my date tonight,*" Vincent replied.

He was too sweet. I hoped whatever Callie was thinking would work.

About forty minutes later she sent me a message. "*Let us in through the back.*"

Us? What was she doing? I scurried downstairs but paused before I turned the corner at the bottom.

"That's a terrible rumor!" I could hear Diamond complain. "How can the prince have a date to the dance? He better not, otherwise that bitch needs to go."

Classy as usual. I rolled my eyes at her statement but waited to see what else she'd say. I didn't want her to know I was up to anything.

"Right?" Rose said in her overly bubbly voice. "It's like so lame. I hope it's wrong. You'd totes be the cutest pair at the dance!"

"Exactly. We'll have to see when I get there. Come on," Diamond replied.

After a moment, I peaked around and was glad to see they had actually left. Relieved, I went to let Callie and whoever else 'us' was in. When I opened the door she was standing there with an open box of fabric and a rolling suitcase of who knows what else.

"Well, let's do this." She nodded for me to move.

I stood back to let her in, and her two friends I recognized from around school. Nola had deep, neon pink hair that was braided back. She lugged in another series of boxes, followed quickly behind by Jasper who gave me a wink.

"You're going to love what we've got planned," he said, trying to shove tulle back into the overflowing box he carried.

"What do you have planned?" I asked, wondering how much stuff they brought along.

His dark eyes met mine. "Miracles."

With nothing more to do, I shut the door and followed them up the stairs.

Callie had already shoved everything off my coffee table and set up a sewing machine. Nola was carefully walking around the room and one by one the pieces of the tattered dress were floating up to follow her. Jasper dumped his box on my bed and began sorting through the materials he had brought.

"I think the original is a goner." Nola gave a sad sigh. "Such a pretty color, too."

"Right? Someday I'll get my vengeance, but for now, we'll create something even better." Callie's eyes seemed to be glowing from magic. "Jasper, are you ready?"

"Can we use a little glitter?" he asked in reply.

"Of course. What's a princess without some sparkle?" Callie smiled at me. "Arnessa, get your hair dried up and change into something a little more form-fitting. We'll totally make this dance, but it'll be just on time at best."

Not wanting to argue with her while she was in the zone, I followed Callie's orders. After I finished, I sat off to the side not wanting to get in the way of the trio's magic. Instead, I sent Vincent a message. *"Callie's got this. There's no way I can meet up early, though."*

"That sucks. I need to be here a little early too."

"I'll meet you there. Promise." With everyone's help, there was no way I'd let Diamond win this one.

The hours went by quickly. Jasper put the finishing touches on the dress and Nola did an amazing job turning my hair into something out of a fairytale. Not to mention my makeup was out of this world. I looked exactly like a princess. While I twirled around in front of the mirror, the other three finished getting ready.

"I don't think we've done something like this in forever." Callie just about skipped over to me. The reds in her dress were an excellent compliment to the deep greens in mine.

"You're amazing. I have no idea how you pulled this plan together so fast." I couldn't stop smiling. The dress fit perfectly. The mixture of skill, luck, and sewing magic really had saved the day.

"We owed her a few favors." Nola laughed.

"And everyone needs a fairy god-makeover once in awhile," Jasper added.

I turned to see his fantastic suit jacket. The deep red wine color glittered as he moved. The cotton broadcloth mix was stunning, jaw-dropping even. The fact I even knew what it was made of told me I actually had taken in some of Callie's ramblings over the years.

I glanced into the mirror once more and admired how the sleeves hung just off the shoulders. The neckline, I was told, was scalloped lace, as was the bodice. The skirt was tulle with slight lace accents toward the bottom with glitter. It looked gorgeous when I spun around. I could not help but giggle in delight before turning back to the others.

Nola turned her hair from neon pink to a more cotton candy shade to better match her dress. "So, are we going to make a grand entrance now or what?"

"Let's," Callie agreed as she looped her arm through mine. "We'll be the best-dressed group there."

The parking lot was packed, but I was fine with the walk thanks to the gorgeous glittery silver flats Callie had brought me. Together, we had to have looked like models walking in. While everyone around us was dressed their best, these fashion students were runway ready. It almost felt like I was sneaking into something big, hidden among the trio.

As soon as we were inside the gym, I could feel the tension melt away from my shoulders. I did it. I actually somehow made it here. I glanced around, lingering in the doorway for a moment before Callie grabbed my hand.

"Let's go find your guy." She smiled, and I let her drag me into the room full of booming music and dim lights.

"There's so many people... I've no idea how we'll find him." I let her lead the way while I tried to figure out this crowd. I had forgotten about the mask part of the masquerade, but it hardly mattered. Only about half of the people followed the theme anyway.

"Found him." Callie finally smirked, pointing up towards the small stage setup.

Stunned, I looked from Vincent to Callie. He wasn't in his normal illusion, instead he was exactly as I saw him last night. The facts all lined up in my head. A royal pain indeed.

"You knew?" I didn't try and hide my shock.

"Best secret I've ever kept." She smirked.

"What do I do?" I wasn't sure how to react. "Like, yes, he's Vincent, but… a prince?" Diamond was going to kill me. Maybe even resurrect me and kill me again.

"Don't worry about them." Callie gave me a reassuring hug. She knew my fears too well. "Dance the night away. They won't even be able to get close."

"But–"

She cut me off. "No buts. Do you think he'd let anything happen tonight, or even after?" Her glare told me she was ready for any argument I could muster up. Instead of trying, I just shook my head. "Exactly."

"I don't know what to do now," I replied lamely.

Callie glanced over at the stage. "We'll just have to magic his attention." She smirked, and before I could protest I could feel her let loose a tendril of magic his way.

Instantly, he glanced over and excused himself from the conversation he was having. Curious eyes watched him walk down from the stage and over to us.

"I was hoping you'd make it." He smiled at us. The happiness in his voice was enough to make me smile.

"I can't believe I didn't get any of your stupid hints." I laughed. They were too blunt to make sense at the time, and now...

Callie took a step back. "And I, for once, didn't ruin the surprise." She winked at me.

"Might have been nice to know a smidge sooner." I couldn't help but laugh more.

"So, you'll still dance with me, then?" he asked hesitantly.

"Of course. You're still Vincent, right?"

"Yes, I am." The relief in his face was instant. "Can you stand one more surprise?"

"I don't think you can possibly top this one, so why not?" Silly boys and their surprises.

Or could he? Without another moment's hesitation he got down on one knee and pulled out a small box. "Would you marry me?"

Somewhere in the background, I heard someone screaming no. It was quickly muffled by a thunderous applause. I stood there in shock for a moment before frantically nodding my approval. "Yes." I was just about in tears from excitement. As he put the ring on my finger I glanced over at Callie who was smirking away knowingly. She knew!

"I guess I was wrong. You could top it." I hugged him tightly, hardly caring that we were the center of attention.

He held me tightly. "Anything for you."

We pulled away from each other, still smiling widely. And I knew that this was exactly how happily ever afters began.

Acknowledgements

Aud: Thank you for continuing to be an awesome beta, supporter, and outstanding friend. I'm glad to have you at my side.

Nichole: It was wonderful being able to have you beta. I loved the comments!

Jasper: This book probably needs more glitter. Book you was a blast to have. Thanks for making an appearance.

Crystalyn: I hope you enjoy book you making it to the ball! You made this so much fun to write.

Steph: I'm so amused that book you got a job at a coffee shop before real you. It would be extra cool if you could brew magic into your lattes.

Liz: Years ago you said something so hilarious to me that it made it into this book. I'm not going to say what though. Just going to low key troll and laugh while you look.

About The Author

Jessica is a fantasy author who formed a love of reading at a young age. While unicorns and magic sparked an interest in the genre, it was childhood friends that convinced her to write. When not dreaming up new adventures, Jessica also enjoys video games, board game nights, and sending bad jokes to friends.

Her author page can be found at:
https://www.facebook.com/authorJEMueller

Made in the USA
Lexington, KY
15 August 2018